THE
LAST GREAT
GETAWAY

of the

WATER BALLOON BOYS

THE
LAST GREAT
GETAWAY
of the
WATER BALLOON BOYS

SCOTT WILLIAM CARTER

SIMON & SCHUSTER BFYR

NEW YORK   LONDON   TORONTO   SYDNEY

for Heidi,
who always believed

SIMON & SCHUSTER BFYR
An imprint of Simon & Schuster Children's Publishing Division
1230 Avenue of the Americas, New York, New York 10020

SIMON & SCHUSTER BFYR
is a trademark of Simon & Schuster, Inc.
For information about special discounts for bulk purchases,
please contact Simon & Schuster Special Sales at
1-866-506-1949 or business@simonandschuster.com.
The Simon & Schuster Speakers Bureau can bring authors to your live event.
For more information or to book an event, contact the Simon & Schuster Speakers
Bureau at 1-866-248-3049 or visit our website at www.simonspeakers.com.
Book design by Tom Daly
The text for this book is set in Gilgamesh.
Manufactured in the United States of America
2 4 6 8 10 9 7 5 3 1
Library of Congress Cataloging-in-Publication Data
Carter, Scott William.
The last great getaway of the Water Balloon Boys / Scott William Carter. — 1st ed.
p. cm.
Summary: When sixteen-year-old Charlie, an excellent student, and his former
best friend Jake take off on an ill-conceived trip from Oregon to Denver in
their principal's car, the results of the choices they make while on the road have
profound effects on both their futures.
ISBN 978-1-4169-7156-6 (hardcover)
[1. Coming of age—Fiction. 2. Conduct of life—Fiction. 3. Voyages and travels—
Fiction. 4. Friendship—Fiction. 5. Crime—Fiction.] I. Title.
PZ7.C2482Las 2010
[Fic]—dc22
2008052423
ISBN 978-1-4169-8250-0 (eBook)

FIRST
EDITION

Acknowledgments

There is no way to thank all the people who helped make the publication of this book possible, but I'd like to single out a few. Special thanks to David Gale and Navah Wolfe, the best editors a first-time novelist could have. To Rachel Vater, my incomparable literary agent, for staying up until the wee hours of the morning reading it that first time—I couldn't have signed with anyone else after that. Both thanks and admiration to Kristine Kathryn Rusch and Dean Wesley Smith, consummate professionals, and the greatest mentors a writer could ever have. Thank you to all the attendees of the OCPFW novel workshop, especially Phaedra Weldon and Leslie Claire Walker. To my parents, for never discouraging my daydreaming. And of course, my eternal gratitude to my first reader and the love of my life, Heidi Carter, for both her unflagging enthusiasm and her unflinching honesty on not just this manuscript, but on all of my writing; I needed both, honey. Thank you.

chapter one

If I'm going to tell you how I killed this kid,

I can't start on the day it happened. It won't make any sense, and you'll just think I was some psycho teenage boy with glue for brains. No, the whole thing really started three days earlier, on Monday, which made it bad straight off. It was also raining, which made it even worse.

In fact, it was raining so hard that my tennis shoes were soaked before I even walked two blocks from our house. Not just kind of wet, either, but really soaked in that way your socks get all squishy and your feet make those mucky sounds each time you take a step. *Muck, muck, muck*, all through the halls, everybody staring at you like you've just turned into a human squid. Back then, before all the crazy stuff happened, most kids looked at me as if I was a human squid anyway. I figured that's what they'd put in the senior yearbook, if they remembered to put anything in there about me at all: *Charlie Hill, Most Likely to Be a Human Squid for the Rest of His Life.*

If it sounds bad, that's because it was. If you want to read a nice, happy little story where everything turns out all neat and tidy in the end, you should go read some Hardy Boys or something. This isn't that kind of story.

Not that *everything* that happened that Monday was bad. About halfway to the school, I realized I had probably missed the bus on purpose.

Somewhere in the foggy parts of my brain I must have known that getting on the bus meant I was also going to get *off* the bus, and that there was a very good chance Leo Gonzalez would be waiting for me when I did. He may not have had brains, but he wasn't the sort of guy who told you he was going to rip off your face and feed it to his gerbils unless he was really going to do it. So missing the bus meant that I was going to be late for school, but it also meant I wouldn't show up when and where he'd expect me.

It was the first thing that morning that made me smile.

People driving to work must have thought I looked pretty strange, squishing along like a human squid, a big smile on my face.

It didn't last long, though. I was still pretty certain I was going to get my face ripped off at some point that day, and it was hard to smile for long when you were wondering how you were going to look with no face.

The rain was not the first bad thing to happen to me that Monday. The first bad thing was when I came down that morning and there was Mom sitting at the kitchen table with her boyfriend, Rick the Accountant, holding hands, both of them smiling like two people in a Viagra commercial.

I was already worried about Leo, and them smiling at me just made me even more worried. They had all the blinds open, and it was so bright my eyes watered, so bright no sane person would have thought it would be raining in less than half an hour.

"Sleep well, sport?" Rick said.

"Uh-huh," I said, rooting around in the cabinet for a Pop-Tart. I tried not to actually speak words to him.

10

"Big day at school?" he said. "How's the prom? Got a date lined up?"

"Whatever," I said.

"Honey, be nice," Mom said. "Rick has something important to say."

I was biting down into a strawberry Pop-Tart, my back to them, and Mom's tone made me freeze. Oh God, I thought, they were getting married. For the rest of my childhood, I'd have to listen to Rick the Accountant calling me sport. I was already sixteen, and really only a year and a half away from freedom on account of me being bumped up a grade when I was eight, but a year seemed like a hell of a long time to be called sport every day.

I felt a little like Mom had just pointed a gun at my back and said, "Stick 'em up." Slowly, waiting for the bullet that would change the rest of my life, I turned around.

Mom already looked like Martha Stewart, so much that people sometimes asked her in the supermarket for decorating advice, but sitting right behind the vase of fresh roses (no doubt Rick's doing), she looked even more like Martha. Rick was smiling, but he had one of those smiles that made him look like he was in pain. With his narrow face, tiny eyes, and slicked-back brown hair, he reminded me of a ferret.

"Well, sport," he said. "I was wondering, well . . ." He looked at Mom.

She gave his hand a reassuring squeeze. "Go ahead, dear."

"Yes, well, it seems you and I have never had the privilege of spending any time together. And I thought, if you were game, you might like to . . . uh, accompany me on a little outing. So we can get to know each other a little. Just the two of us."

It was like he was speaking Martian. "Huh?" I said.

"He wants to know if you want to go camping with him, dear," Mom said.

"Yes, right," Rick said. "That's it exactly. Just somewhere in western Oregon. Not too far."

"Camping?" I said. "Like, in a tent?"

"Sure, sure," Rick said.

"In the outdoors and everything?"

"Of course, of course."

"But why?"

Rick was a pretty unflappable guy, but this seemed to confuse him. He looked at Mom, who smiled at him reassuringly, then gave me one of those *now I'm going to explain it all so you can understand it* looks of hers.

"I thought it would be a good idea, dear," she said.

"Okay."

"You two should get to know each other better."

"Okay."

"It'd make me happy. You see, Rick and I are getting married."

Pow. Mom fired the gun after all.

I reached the gray slab of concrete that was West Rexton High at five after eight, which meant I was twenty minutes late. I've seen a lot of ugly buildings over the years, but I'd still say our school was the ugliest one ever constructed. It looked like someone had started to design a building that was merely ugly, then got depressed halfway

4

through at how ugly it was and gave up, making it look not only ugly, but ugly and unfinished. There was gray concrete, rusting steel-rimmed windows, and scuffed-up metal doors on all sides.

The rain let up right when I reached the school. It couldn't have been timed any better to make sure I received maximum soakage. Standing there, my hand on the cold door handle, my heart was pounding so hard I thought I might pass out. Leo could be lurking anywhere. When I was sure no one was looking, I opened the door and hurried down the shadowy hallway lined with lockers, ducking under the windows on the doors of each classroom, until I reached the boys' bathroom. *Muck, muck, muck,* my soggy shoes were so loud on the tiles I cringed with each step.

Luckily, nobody was in there. The bathroom was divided into two rooms, the outer one for the circular sink, the inner one for the urinals and the toilets, a swinging door separating them. I went into the first stall, slipped off my backpack, and sat down on the edge of the toilet seat with the backpack on my lap.

My clothes felt like they were glued to my skin. Now all I had to do was wait twenty minutes until the bell rang, then I could just go to second period along with everybody else. I'd have an "unexcused absence" to explain to Mom later, which was worse than being tardy, but it was better than going to first period so late. If I did that, Mrs. Ameson would give me *the look.* You know the one. The one people give you when they're disappointed in you, and those looks absolutely killed me. I did everything I could to avoid them.

Thinking about Mom made me think about the wedding, and that got me even more depressed. I spent most of my time either depressed or really depressed, and you wouldn't think there'd be much of a difference between the two, but there really was. It was the difference between being just mildly annoyed at how sucky my life was and really truly angry about it. You could get through the day without too much trouble being mildly annoyed, but it's like trying to walk underwater when you're angry all the time.

To take my mind off Mom and Rick, I decided to maybe do some studying, and thinking about homework made me remember the portrait. Dad's portrait. The one Mrs. Morchester had assigned, telling us to draw a picture of somebody in your family. I used the picture on the Christmas postcard he'd sent me two years back, the one with him, "the ditzy hygienist slut who was the flavor of the month" (which was what Mom called her, despite the fact that this woman had appeared on Dad's Christmas cards several years in a row), and the two black labs wearing red Santa hats. I would have used the Christmas card from *this* year, but Dad had sent a lame *Garfield* card (does *anyone* read *Garfield* anymore?) with no picture inside.

Even though the assignment wasn't due for a week, the thought of it being ruined terrified me because I actually thought it was decent. Not great, but decent, and I hardly ever thought the stuff I drew was any good. My hands were shaking as I searched through the backpack and located my blue drawing pad. The cover felt cold, but not wet. I opened it, flipped past pages and pages of stupid cartoons, robots, and sword-and-sorcery stuff, and finally located Dad's portrait, breathing a sigh when I saw it wasn't ruined.

It suddenly occurred to me that I really had to go to the bathroom. I had been so worried about the drawing I hadn't noticed until the pressure was really intense. I put away the drawing pad, then started to unbutton my pants. That's when I heard the outer bathroom door swing open.

"That Haines is a total loser."

"Yeah, yeah, a loser. Totally."

I recognized the voices, and the pressure down below became a lot more intense. It was none other than Leo Gonzalez, the kid destined to rip off my face, and his friend Parrot Pete. Everybody called him Parrot Pete, because that's all he did, repeat things.

"I gotta take a piss," Leo said.

"Yeah, a piss," Parrot Pete said.

Sneakers squeaked on the tiles. Right before the door banged open, I lifted my feet and pressed them against the back of the stall door so they were out of sight. There was more shoe squeaking, the sounds of flies being unzipped, and the trickle of water. There was one flush, then two. I sat there praying for them to leave, but there was no swinging door, no footsteps. Instead, I heard the rustle of clothing.

"You want one?" Leo said.

"Sure, yeah."

"Figure we got a few minutes before Haines misses us."

Mr. Haines was the shop teacher. I heard the sound of a lighter, then saw smoke rising over the top of the stall. I couldn't hold my breath any longer, so as quietly as I could, I let it out and breathed in through my mouth. I was afraid to breathe through my nose because if I did, I might sneeze, and then that would be the end of my time on Earth as a face-bearing person.

"Camels are the best, man," Leo said.

"Yeah, the best," Parrot Pete said.

"Hey, you seen that prick Charlie Hill around this morning?"

"Nah," Parrot Pete said.

"Bet the little dickwad didn't even come to school. What a little dickwad. I really scared him on Friday. I could tell. You should have seen his face. He looked like a scared little dickwad. Probably at home crapping his pants."

Because I was so close to nearly making his guess real, I half wondered if he knew where I was. I wasn't much of a God-believing person—I always figured that if he *did* exist, there wouldn't be people like Leo Gonzalez in the world—but I did a fair amount of praying right about then. I figured if somehow I was wrong about God, then it wouldn't hurt to hedge my bets and tell him I'd donate a bunch of money to nuns if he could just get me out of this without them finding me.

"Dickwad's probably at home crapping his pants," Parrot Pete said.

"I already said that, man," Leo said. Even he could get irritated at Pete.

"Right, sorry."

"It's like, nobody messes with my girl, you know?" Leo said. "I can't believe that little prick. It's like, how could he not know she was mine? Everybody knows Tessa is mine."

"Everybody knows it," Parrot Pete agreed.

They puffed away in silence for a while, me enduring my private agony. The cigarette smoke was now so strong that my eyes stung. I heard the outer bathroom door swing open. Leo and Parrot Pete must have heard it too because I heard them crash into a stall a couple down. There was flushing. The swinging door opened.

"Aw, man," Leo said. "I thought maybe you was the principal. You coulda said something. We lost two smokes."

"Sorry."

The voice sounded familiar. I heard more unzipping, the tinkle of piss hitting the porcelain.

"Well, we better get back," Leo said.

"Yeah, we better," Parrot Pete said.

"Hey, wait a minute. Dude, you seen that little prick kid, Charlie Hill, around?"

There was a pause just long enough that I felt a sinking feeling in my stomach.

"Nope."

"Damn. Well, I'm gonna get him. He has to come to school eventually."

"Why?"

"Huh?"

"Why do you want to get him?"

Then, while Leo must have been struggling with the question, it hit me: The voice belonged to Jake Tucker. Jake, who used to be my neighbor until my family bought a house and moved in the middle of sixth grade. Jake, who had been my best friend for years, especially in the summer, when we'd hang out in the fort Dad had built until one of us got called home for dinner. Jake, who broke my Game Boy when he borrowed it, then refused to admit it, saying it was broken when I gave it to him. It happened right before we moved. Months later, he called and left a message with Mom, but I never called him back. We hadn't spoken since, both of us avoiding each other's eyes in the hall for a couple of years, until eventually we didn't have to avoid each other's eyes because we were pretty much strangers to each other.

Not that I passed him in the halls all that often. He wasn't at school much, getting suspended for one reason or another. Smoking. Pulling pranks. I'd heard he hung out at the pool hall downtown. I knew his dad had left when he was about thirteen, but I'd also heard his mom had become a meth addict shortly after his dad left and that she now mostly lived on the streets. Jake's foster parents were kind of shady people too. Real great life.

"Huh?" Leo eventually responded.

"I said, 'Why do you want to get him?'"

"What's it to you?"

"Just asking."

Another pause. "Well, mind your own business."

"Whatever," Jake said, and you had to admire the calm in his voice. He didn't sound worried at all, even though I'm sure Leo outweighed him by fifty pounds. Jake wasn't a big guy, if I remembered correctly. Tall, but kind of thin. "Can I bum a smoke off you?"

"Screw you," Leo said.

"Yeah, screw you," Parrot Pete said.

"Shut up, Pete."

"Right, sorry."

The swinging door opened. I heard the squeak of footsteps. I wasn't sure if all of them had left, or just Leo and Pete, so I waited. If it was between my life and clean underwear, I'd take my life.

"You can come out now," Jake said.

chapter two

When you have to go to the bathroom, there
comes a point when your willpower has been stretched to the limit.
There're literally tears in your eyes, you want to go so bad. It's like
a near-death experience. You might see yourself in a dark tunnel, a
light at the end. Maybe you hear angels singing. You're balancing
on the edge of a cliff, and the slightest little thing could push you
off. Anything. A little breeze. The brush of a feather. Maybe even a
loud thought. That's where I was: right at the edge.

Jake's voice startled me, and I dropped my backpack onto the
floor. But I didn't go over the edge. My resolve held. I found out
that day I had titanium intestines. A bladder of steel. It wasn't the
sort of thing you'd put on a college application, but it was a good
thing to know.

I snatched up the backpack and emerged from the stall, trying
not to look as uncomfortable as I felt.

He stood by the far window, arms crossed, a smirk on his face.
He was a real smirking kind of guy. His blond hair was long and
greasy, coming down nearly to his shoulders. Some guys looked
good with long hair, but Jake didn't. He just looked like a guy
who needed a haircut. He wore faded and ripped jeans and a jean
jacket, over a plain white T-shirt with holes that looked like they'd
been caused by cigarette burns. In all the times I had seen him
at high school, I'd never seen him wear anything else. He wore

the jean jacket even when it was a hundred degrees outside.

My guess was it was because he wanted to look bigger. He was so thin that if he turned sideways, you might mistake him for a graham cracker. I was pretty thin myself, but I was Fat Albert standing next to him.

The rainy-day light from the window made his skin look kind of gray. It was pockmarked, too, like he'd used his face as an ashtray. I remembered him having really bad acne our freshman year, but now it was just craters and divots. It didn't make him look ugly, though. It made him look kinda badass, like he'd done and seen a lot; and from the way girls talked about him, it seemed they liked that sort of thing. He was only a year older than me, but he could have passed for twenty-one while I still sometimes got carded at a PG-13 movie.

"Hey," I said.

"Hey."

"How'd you know I was in there?"

He snorted. "Not everybody is as stupid as those two. Your muddy footprints—they still look fresh. And I also saw you walk into the school a few minutes ago. Figured it's where you'd go."

"Oh," I said.

There was a pause. I didn't know what else to say, and besides, I couldn't really concentrate. It took all of my concentration to keep from filling my pants. The only thing that came to mind was how he broke my Game Boy. I wondered if he was thinking about the Game Boy, too. You'd think after so many years, you'd forget about something like that, but it still made me mad, thinking about it. I really loved that Game Boy.

"So'd you do it?" he asked.

"Do what?"

"Do what they're saying you did."

"What're they saying?"

"That you put a love note in Tessa Boone's locker."

I swallowed. I was trying to think of what to say when the first bell rang, making me jump, and I nearly had an accident right there.

"You shouldn't believe everything people say," I said.

I pushed through the swinging door. Other kids were already entering.

"Hey," he said.

"What?" I said, holding the door open. I expected more of the Spanish Inquisition from him.

He pointed at my pants. "You may want to button up before you go out there. Just saying."

As soon as I left the bathroom, the first place I went was to the bathroom on the second floor. It wasn't like I could just go back into the stall after I had made such a big deal of leaving the way I did.

Somehow I managed to avoid Leo the rest of the day, though it wasn't easy. Parrot Pete saw me at lunch when I was hunkering down in the art room, his eyes getting all big and wide, but I practically glued myself to Mrs. Morchester. It was pretty easy to glue myself to her, because by early afternoon I still hadn't fully dried yet. I also passed Tessa Boone's locker once. She was tall and blond, taller than most boys, actually, and she was wearing her blue-and-white cheerleader's getup. She had her back to me, so I thought I might slip past so she didn't see me (pretty stupid thought, really, when you're a squeaky human squid), but one of her girlfriends heard my squishing sneakers and giggled. There were three other girls gathered around Tessa, and soon they were all staring at me and giggling. Tessa looked over her shoulder, saw me, and looked away quickly. Her neck reddened. Soon everybody in the hall was staring and giggling, one big happy staring and giggling fest.

Somehow I made it to sixth period, Advanced Economics, with my face still attached. The problem was I was pretty certain that when the bell went off, Leo, Parrot Pete, and maybe some of their other goons would make a point of being outside waiting for me. I could pretty much guarantee it. What I did was wait until five after two, about ten minutes before last bell, then asked Mr. Edwards if I could go to the bathroom.

I took my backpack, which made him raise his eyebrows, but he didn't stop me. Teachers really will trust you to the limit until you give them reason not to, so I was glad, for once, that I had always been a good student. I headed for the nearest exit—the one that led out to the track field—and was nearly to the door when the worst possible thing happened. Mr. Harkin—our huge, bald ex-Marine principal—backed out of one of the rooms into my path.

There was half a second when I thought I might be able to skate past him before he saw me, and I veered to the far wall, but he turned too fast.

"Charles," he said.

He had one of those Darth Vader voices, so deep that he some-times made the freshman girls cry by just asking for their hall passes. There was no way to just keep walking once he spoke to you. I couldn't even muster any irritation at him using my full name.

"Yes sir," I said.

"How're you doing, son?" he said. "You having a good day?"

I had expected him to ask for my hall pass, but apparently even Mr. Harkin trusted me completely. I never wanted to be in a position where he caught me lying. There were rumors that he had killed people in Vietnam with his bare hands. Lots of them. And that he had enjoyed it.

"Yes sir," I said.

"You picked out a college yet, son?"

"No sir."

"Well, you should start thinking about it. Next year you'll be a senior, and it won't be long before you move on to greener pastures. You should be able to get plenty of scholarships. Your test scores and your grades put you right at the top of the class. Did you know that?"

"Um, no sir. I mean, well, yes sir, I know I've done kinda well." I glanced at the exit down the hall. The bell would ring any moment, and that door was so far away. It was like in another time zone.

"I spoke to your mom when she was here on Parent Day," Mr. Harkin said. "She said you want to be a doctor."

"Yes sir."

"That's great. Being a doctor is a good calling. I know your father is a doctor. Or a dentist." He laughed. "Same thing, I guess."

I wasn't expecting him to bring up Dad, and I glanced up at him, trying to read his expression. He had that concerned look adults get when they're trying to be adults who know better than kids.

"Yes sir," I said.

He looked at me for a long time, and I thought, here it comes, he's going to try to tell me how the divorce wasn't my fault, that these things happen, that both my parents love me and that's all that really matters, stuff I'd heard a million times in the last four years. It was the kind of thing some people have to say to make themselves feel like everything's okay, that kids who go through divorces aren't royally screwed, when they know, deep down, that they probably are.

"Well, you know, son, divorce happens," he said. "It wasn't your fault at all. You know that. You just keep on doing well and great things will happen for you."

I felt like a deflating balloon. Even though I *knew* he was going to say something like that, it didn't stop me from hoping he wouldn't.

"Yes sir."

The bell rang, and I'm sure my heart must have stopped. I had maybe five seconds before kids starting spilling into the hall. The room doors were opening. I turned to go, but Mr. Harkin wasn't quite done with me.

"Oh, and that was a good choice," he said.

"Huh? I mean, sorry sir?"

He chuckled. "I heard you asked Tessa Boone to the prom." He winked at me and strode away.

The level of mortification I had reached in that moment, the pure and utter humiliation that filled every cell in my body knowing that the rumor about me and Tessa had reached even

Mr. Harkin, who truly was the last person in the school to find out about anything, was so great, so overpowering, that I literally could not move for a good ten seconds. Looking back, those ten seconds may have made all the difference.

Kids filled the hall, streaming around me. Laughter and voices echoed off the tiles. Finally, I snapped out of it and bolted for the door. With so many human obstacles in the way, it took forever before I finally pushed through the doors and made it outside.

The sky was a strange shimmering color of blue, like the color of our dish detergent, and the air felt cool and moist. The way home was across the parking lot and down the steps to the track field, and then to the other side and Warren Street. I thought I had a pretty good head start, but I was just across the parking lot when I heard a shout.

"Hey!"

It was Leo. I looked over my shoulder and saw him standing on the steps outside the school—him, Parrot Pete, and two football-type guys who could each probably squash me with their pinkie fingers.

There were maybe three or four seconds when we just stared at each other across the glistening asphalt, the predator and the prey, the bully and the abused, the football star and the grade A geek, and then finally Leo grinned and the spell was broken.

I ran.

With lots of whooping and hollering, they ran after me.

I knew there was absolutely no chance I could outrun them. I knew it in the same way a rabbit knows he can't outrun the hawk he's just spotted swooping down on him. I knew it, and yet I ran, anyway, just like the rabbit runs. We may be a lot smarter than rabbits (of course, if you put up Leo as the comparison study, it's a close call), but when it comes to the fight or flight response, we're no different.

Me, I was all about flight.

When you weighed 120 pounds, and you couldn't even bench-press volume *Z* of the *Encyclopedia Britannica*, you didn't have a choice.

Down the stairs. Tripped at the bottom. Scraped my hands on the concrete. Back up, running like a madman across the rust-colored Astroturf track, my sneakers like wet sponges. Now onto the grass in the center. *Squish, squish,* the grass was wet. But couldn't slow down. Halfway across, I glanced over my shoulder and saw them at the bottom of the stairs.

"Gonna get you, loser!" Leo cried.

"Yeah, gonna get you!" Parrot Pete said.

Faster, faster, lungs burning. Had to keep pushing myself. Run, rabbit, run. Then tragedy struck.

My foot came down in a bald spot in the grass, and because the ground was wet, the mud acted like a suction cup on my shoe, pulling it clean off. I took a couple of tumbling steps before finally crashing. Wet grass went into my mouth and up my nose. I heard laughter. Then I was up and running, leaving the other shoe behind. I managed only a couple of steps before going down again. This time the laughter was closer.

I struggled to my feet, but someone gave me a hard kick on the butt and I went down face first in the grass. More laughter. Shadows fell across me.

"Get up, faggot," Leo said.

"Yeah, yeah, get up," Parrot Pete said.

The two other guys offered up something equally memorable. Everybody was pulling for me to get up, my own private booster squad. I opted for playing dead, lying there facedown. I heard it sometimes worked on bears. Unfortunately, it didn't work on Leo. He gave me a swift kick in the gut. I saw sunbursts on the backs of my eyelids. I rolled onto my side, in the fetal position, hugging myself.

"Up," Leo said.

All I could manage was a groan. Leo's buddies grabbed me and hoisted me up. My vision was blurred with both water and tears, and I blinked, trying to see. Leo was nothing but a streak of black hair and a Cheshire cat grin. My side throbbed.

"Why'd you write Tessa that note?" Leo asked.

"I—I didn't—" I began.

He punched me in the gut. This one knocked the wind out of me, and I doubled over, coughing.

"Why'd you write the note?" Leo asked again.

"I'm sorry," I managed. "I didn't mean anything."

"I don't give a rat's ass if you're sorry," Leo said. "I wanna know why you wrote it. Did you think I wouldn't find out?"

"I—I—"

"You think I'm stupid, that it?"

"N-no—"

"And why'd you even think she'd be interested in a total loser like you?"

"I'm sorry."

"Shut up!"

"Okay, okay," I said, still hoping I might be able to talk myself out of this one, "listen, I'm just—"

He hit me in the face. At least I think he hit me in the face. The next thing I knew, I was on the ground. I felt a trickle in my nose, and I tasted blood in my mouth. My ears rang like church bells. The goons lifted me up again, and this time I hung limp, defeated, knowing that he was just going to pummel me until there was nothing left of me but a pulp. Charlie Hill, the human pulp. It was going to be brutal.

"Look at me," he said.

Slowly, I lifted my head. He was smiling with glee.

"I gotta make a 'zample out of you," he said. "I can't have people going after my girl. I can't have them thinking I won't do nothing."

I didn't answer. What was I going to say? I could try to fight, but I figured that would just make it so much worse for me in the end. He pulled his fist back, and it looked as big as anything I'd seen before in my life. This was Mount Rushmore, or the Great Wall of China. I'd like to say I saw my life flash before my eyes, but it wasn't anything like that. It was just me standing in one shoe and one soggy sock, a lot of pain in my gut, and his giant fist cocking like a big gun.

Then a bomb went off.

That's what it sounded like, and we all jerked and dropped into a crouch. I turned and looked in the direction of the sound, and it took my mind a moment to make sense of what it was seeing. It was as if the spaceship from *E.T.* dropped down right in the middle of *Dances with Wolves*. You just don't expect it, and it takes you a while to even see what it is. A large red beast had just flattened a huge section of chain-link fence and was charging toward us.

No.

Not a beast.

A car. Not just any car. Mr. Harkin's cherry red '67 Mustang, the very same car our principal parked right outside his office so that he could look on it lovingly all day long. The very same car that no senior class had dared to involve in any pranks, when just about everything else was fair game. Rumor had it that about five years earlier a biology teacher had scratched the Mustang's door while carrying a box of bunsen burners, and that teacher was now teaching in Barrow, Alaska, where the sun didn't even rise a month out of the year. Nobody touched Mr. Harkin's Mustang.

And yet, there in the driver's seat was Jake Tucker, my old neighbor, once a pal and then a Game Boy breaker, barreling toward us. The top of the Mustang was down, and his blond hair billowed in the wind. His mirrored sunglasses flashed in the sunlight.

For a moment, it didn't look like he was going to slow down, and my captors edged away from me. Then the Mustang spun to the right, spitting grass and dirt right at my feet. At the same time, while the Mustang spun, the passenger door flew open. Then the car was stopped, engine idling, and Jake stared out at me with his mirrored sunglasses and his sly smirk.

"You getting in?" he said.

None of us moved. It was all too surreal. But then I realized I had a choice, and I had only a few seconds, while Leo and his friends were still too stunned to grab me, to make it. There are moments when your life spins on a wheel, when the choices you make forever change the person you are and the person you will become. I could stay and get pulverized by Leo and his friends, or I could escape in the Mustang only to meet my certain doom later at the hands of Mr. Harkin. Leo's fist now, or Harkin's wrath later—which was worse? Looking back, it seems like there might have been other options available to me, but those were the only two roads I could see.

I got into the car.

chapter three

With a laugh, Jake put it in gear and we sped across the field, over the broken fence, tires squealing on asphalt. It had all happened so fast I hardly had time to blink. I saw kids along the street, backpacks and books in tow, everybody lined up and watching us as if we were the first float in a parade. One block passed, then another, neither of us speaking. My own mind raced as I tried to imagine how I was going to get out of this mess without getting expelled. I was in Mr. Harkin's car. Without his permission. And dozens of people had just witnessed it. I was no expert on the law, but I was pretty sure that would qualify as auto theft.

Forget being expelled. I was hoping I didn't end up in prison. This was very bad. Very, very bad.

Jake finally turned and looked at me. In the mirrored sunglasses, I saw my own face, and it shocked me. A purple bruise was swelling over my eye, and blood darkened my upper lip and my chin. Then the pain finally registered, as if it had been temporarily left behind and had finally caught up; it felt as if my whole face was throbbing. I tasted blood in my mouth.

"Hey, pal," he said. "Charles. The Chuckster. Chuck the man."

I stared at him, trying to understand how he could joke at a time like this. I should have been grateful that he had saved me from Leo, but all I could think was that he had now ruined my life. The way I saw it, it wasn't like I had *chosen* to get into the Mustang after all. It was more of a self-preservation thing. If he would have just left me alone, I might have gotten my face ripped off, but at least I wouldn't have ended up in jail.

"Charlie," I said.

"Aww, come on," he said. "You know I was just joshing ya."

"It's Charlie."

"Okay, whatever . . . Charlene." He laughed.

I wanted to go on hating him. It was something to focus on other than my pain and my situation. But despite myself, I laughed, and then suddenly it was like old times. "You're such a dork," I said.

He laughed with me. "Double dork."

"Dork on a stick!"

"Dork on a stick with a turd on top!"

And there we were, laughing until tears were in our eyes, two fourth graders in a stolen Mustang who thought there was nothing funnier than potty talk. I laughed until it was no longer funny, and then I laughed some more, because what do you do in a situation like that except laugh? Finally, our laughter died, and then we rode in somber silence, alone with our thoughts, the rumbling motor, and the cool rush of wind. It finally dawned on me that I couldn't go on riding in Mr. Harkin's Mustang forever. Sooner or later I'd have to come to grips with reality, and it would probably be better if it was sooner.

"Better pull over now," I said.

"Pull over?" Jake said.

"Yeah."

"What, you need to take a leak or something?"

14

I touched the bruise over my eye, wincing at the pain. A couple more hours, and the thing would cover my face like a giant wart. "Very funny. What, you think you're just going to keep driving the principal's car all day?"

"Sure. All day. All night. Something like that."

I looked at him. His smirk made it hard to tell if he was joking.

"You're insane," I said.

"Nah, just having some fun."

"Jake, we have to get out *now*."

"Why?"

I couldn't believe he was arguing with me on this. "Why?! Because Mr. Harkin is going to break off all our arms and legs, that's why! If we stop now, maybe we can tell him you were helping me get away from Leo, but if we keep driving—"

"Don't be such a pussy."

It took me a moment to register his insult. "What?"

"A pussy. You're being a total pussy. Have some fun. Jesus."

"Fun!"

"Yeah. You knew how to have fun once."

I stared, incredulous. He wanted to have fun. We were in Mr. Harkin's Mustang, and he thought we should have some fun.

"Okay, I need to get out now," I said.

"Aw," he said.

"I'm serious, Jake. Stop the car."

"In a little bit."

"Jake!"

He smiled. "You wanna drive?"

"No, I don't want to drive!"

"It's a lot of fun. A lot of pep in this baby. My dad had one like this a long time ago. It was yellow, though."

"I don't care! Stop the car!"

Jake drummed his fingers on the steering wheel. We'd gone about a mile from the school, heading out of the residential areas and into the light industrial side of town that surrounded the airport. The buildings were huge and square and gray, one after another. I realized he wasn't driving randomly. He was driving with somewhere in mind.

"Where are you going?" I said.

He looked at me. "Did you write that note to Tessa Boone?"

"What does that have to do with anything?"

"I just wanna know."

I shook my head. "Stop the car, Jake."

"Not until you tell me if you wrote that note."

I put my hand on the door handle. "If you don't stop the car, I'm going to jump out."

"Oh, this should be good," he said.

"Jake, come on!"

He laughed.

"We're in serious trouble here!" I protested.

"You worry too much. What happened to you? You used to be the one who threw the first balloon."

It took me a second to realize what he meant, and then it all came rushing back. I remembered how we used to fill up water balloons and put them into a plastic bucket. I remembered how we had hauled that bucket into the great big pine tree next to our apartment complex, high above the bluff where the complex sat, high enough that we could see Oak Knoll Road over the smaller oak trees. I remembered how we had taken turns lobbing water balloons at passing cars, laughing with delight when one of them hit its mark. I remembered how sometimes the owners would get out, steaming mad, and come looking for us, and how we disappeared through the maze of hedges that surrounded the complex, hiding, stifling our laughter as best we could.

"This is different," I said.

"How is it different?"

"We were just kids then."

"Oh, so you're all grown-up now? Ready to go to some boring job and come home to some boring house and some boring wife and do that again and again?"

"I didn't say that."

"Then lighten up. Have some fun."

I shook my head. "Jake, we're going to get arrested."

"Aw."

"I'm serious."

He looked at me. "I can tell. You get that look on your face."

"What look?"

"That serious look. The Harvard look."

"Harvard!"

"Yeah. Or Yale. Princeton. The serious look of the guy who's going to one of those big-time schools. It's the I'm-going-to-be-a-lawyer-or-doctor look. It's priceless. Hey, you ever seen those MasterCard commercials?"

"What?"

"Those commercials. You ever seen them? They're pretty

good." He changed his voice, making it more smooth. "A cherry-red Mustang and a sunny afternoon . . . priceless."

He started reciting some of his favorite MasterCard commercials, and I just went on staring at him, trying to figure out just what planet his brain was on. How could he not be worried? I realized I was going to have to get out of the car before he did something really insane. Next time he stopped for a traffic light or a stop sign, I'd go for it. That was my plan, but he must have sensed what I was up to, because he only tapped the brakes at the next intersection, screeching around the corner.

"Jake, come on!" I pleaded.

"Just wait," he said.

"I really just want to go home."

"You will. Later. For now you're going to have some fun, whether you want to or not. It's my mission."

"This is *so* not funny."

He burst out laughing. "Oh, but it is. The look on your face . . . priceless."

"Will you stop saying that!"

He was laughing so hard now his face was turning red. He wiped the tears out of his eyes and turned right onto Mission Street, a four-lane road that led past many of the big box stores like Wal-Mart and Target. It may have been my imagination, but everyone in all the cars we passed seemed to reach for cell phones just as they saw us, and I figured they had Mr. Harkin's number on speed dial. Rexton was a decent-size city, over a hundred thousand, but I had no doubt in my mind that everyone knew this car.

I kept waiting for Jake to take one of the exits, but he didn't, and then Mission Street turned into Highway 47, the one that led east out of town. His speed picked up, doing forty, then fifty. I asked him just what he thought he was doing, but he didn't hear me over the roar of the wind, so I had to shout.

"Where are you going?" I said.

His smirk was so small, so tight, you could barely see his lips. "It's a secret."

"Jake . . ."

"All right, all right. We're going to see a friend of mine."

"A friend."

"Yeah. A girl. Lives in Grantville."

"Grantville! That's like twenty miles away!"

"Well, that's where she lives. She goes to high school there. Name's Laurel. You'll like her."

"I don't want to like her!"

"What, you don't like girls? You gay or something?"

"I'm not gay!"

"It's okay if you are. It's not like I hate fags or anything. It's not like I'm prejudiced. It's just, if you're going to try to grab my ass, I'd like to know."

"I'm not gay!"

"Okay, okay," he said. "Then what's the problem? She's got girl-friends. They're hot, too. Maybe not as hot as Tessa Boone, but pretty hot." He winked at me.

"This is insane!"

He laughed. "Yeah, isn't it great? Just like old times."

I thought about telling him we never once stole a car and went for a joyride, but there didn't seem to be any point. He was crazy.

Totally, unbelievably out of his mind. The next twenty minutes, as we raced over the old highway, I tried a few times to get him to stop, but he just laughed.

We passed beyond the Rexton city limits, past the women's state pen and the yellow fields surrounding it, then turned onto the narrower Highway 42, a two-lane road that wound through a tunnel of pines and oaks. We passed several Christmas tree farms, some houses on big acreage with horses grazing out front, and a wrecking yard. Then we passed the Grantville sign, population 6,567, and dropped to a slow cruise as we drove among the brick buildings of the old downtown. A couple of old-timers sitting outside a barber shop stared at us as we passed. It took me a second before I realized one of the older-timers was wearing a police uniform.

"I think I'm going to be sick," I said.

"Relax," Jake said. "If you don't look like you're guilty, nobody will think anything."

We passed through some neighborhoods filled with boxy rundown manufactured homes, then veered sharply into a gravel alley. Overhanging cherry trees lined the way, making the alley cool and shadowy. Fallen cherries had stained the gravel over the years, so it was now more red than gray, as if it was an exposed wound.

We drove past a few backyards, past wild grass, rusted swing sets, and cracked kiddie pools, and then he turned onto a dirt path behind a two-story gray house with cracked windows and red graffiti on the back door. The backyard was filled with junk—the biggest of which was an old VW Bug without wheels or a hood—and also a big, fishing-type boat up on its trailer. The boat was in worse shape than the car, the boards cracked and splintered, the cabin with no glass at all.

There were also small streams of smoke rising out of the darkness of the cabin.

"Something's on fire," I said.

Jake laughed. Right after he killed the engine, a face appeared in one of the glassless windows—a girl with curly red hair tied back in a ponytail. She had pale skin with lots of freckles, like vanilla ice cream with chocolate sprinkles. Her eyes lit up when she saw us.

"Jake!" she exclaimed.

"Hey, Laurel," Jake said. "Like my ride?"

"Your ride?"

"Yeah."

She ducked out of view. I heard her speaking to someone out of sight, then she and another girl emerged on deck. The deck boards creaked like they might give way at any moment.

Laurel wore an acid-burn jean jacket over a softball shirt, as well as dirt-stained white sweatpants. She was a little on the heavy side, but she was still pretty good looking because she had a lot of curves for somebody her age. The other girl looked completely different, one of those goth types dressed all in black. Her hair was black, her eyebrows black, her eyeliner black. Her hair was cut really short, hardly over her ears, and she was very thin, with no breasts at all. In fact, you might have thought her a boy until you got a good look at her face, which was really kind of pretty, if you could get past the eyeliner and the eyebrows. The two girls didn't seem to belong together at all. Athletic types never hung out with goths. It was like trying to mix oil and water.

They scooted off the bow and jumped down to the ground. Both girls held smoldering cigarettes. They approached the car, standing on Jake's side. The goth girl seemed to be trying hard not to make eye contact with Jake or me, as if she was doing her best Dustin Hoffman Rain Man impersonation. Laurel looked at the car a long time, her eyes getting real wide.

"You like?" Jake said.

"Where'd you get this?" she said.

"We stole it," Jake said. "Actually Charlie here stole it. I just went along with him."

"I did not," I said.

Jake laughed. "He just doesn't like to brag. Who's your friend?"

Laurel took a drag from her cigarette. "This is Kari. She just moved here from New Jersey."

"Well hey, Kari," Jake said. "I'm Jake, and this here is Charlie."

Kari was staring at the side of the car, as if there was a scratch there and she was trying to make it go away with her mind.

"What, can't they talk in New Jersey?" Jake said.

"Screw you, asshole," Kari said. She said this without even looking at him.

Laurel looked at her. "Hey, be nice. Jake's a cool guy."

"Whatever," Kari said.

Laurel sighed. "Don't mind her. She just hates everything and everyone. But she's still cool."

"Everything sucks," Kari said. "What happened to your face, anyway?"

She asked this question without glancing in my direction, so it took me a moment to realize that she was asking about me. I'd forgotten for a moment about what a mess Leo had made of my face. I already had a hard enough time talking to girls in general—it was like giving a speech to the entire school, only worse, every single time I tried to open my mouth—and looking so awful only made it worse.

"Oh, I don't know," I said.

"You look like crap," Kari said.

Jake must have thought this was very funny, because he burst into laughter. "Oh, that's great," he said. "Actually, Charlie here was in a pretty bad fight. Took on three guys. You should have seen the wreck he made of them." He whistled. "And all because they insulted this girl he's taking to prom."

For the first time, Kari looked at me. Her eyes, which were actually not black at all—instead, a very light, uneven blue, like water with a few drops of food coloring—seemed very different from the rest of her. It was like there was somebody else inside, somebody really lonely or afraid, and she was doing her best to hide that person behind all her black walls. I wondered if maybe that's why she never wanted to look at anyone directly, because she knew people could see right inside her through her eyes, right into the real her. She looked at me only a moment before looking away.

Laurel was also looking at me, with what seemed newfound admiration. "Seriously?"

"Well . . ." I began.

"He doesn't like to talk about that stuff," Jake said. "He was in a lot of fights when he was little, and he doesn't like to talk about it."

"Oh," Laurel said, nodding.

"Hey, you guys want to go for a ride?"

"Yeah!" Laurel exclaimed.

She ground her cigarette into the dirt with her heel. Then, before I could argue—and really, I wasn't going to argue, because I could hardly speak around girls, and if you can't speak, you can't argue—Laurel climbed into the backseat. Kari climbed in after her, taking her time, like it really didn't matter to her one way or another.

Jake backed out of the alley onto the street. Smiling at us, he revved the engine a few times, then popped it in gear. The tires squealed and the Mustang took off like a rocket.

"Let's have some fun," Jake said.

We were halfway down the street before I realized that I had had all the time in the world to get out of the car, and I hadn't bothered to do it.

We cruised through the side streets until we

ended up in the old downtown, the rumbling motor echoing off the brick buildings. I saw our reflection in some of the store windows, and it was like something out of a James Dean movie, two guys and two girls in a Mustang, cruising for action. There were lots of loitering teenagers down there, mostly loser types, some hanging around the theater or the drugstore, and Laurel laughed and waved to them. Most of them just stared back with blank expressions.

The air had cooled, and a light breeze stirred up the dust from the sidewalks. The clock by the bank showed that it was closing in on four o'clock. Another hour and a half and Mom would be home. When she didn't find me, she'd get worried.

That was, if she wasn't already. Mr. Harkin may have already called her at work. No doubt he knew by now it was me and Jake who took his car. As we rumbled along, I tried to understand why I hadn't gotten out of the car. Jake had stopped at a bunch of stop signs, and I hadn't gotten out at any of those, either. I knew I was *supposed* to get out, that I *had* to get out, and yet I didn't. Something was wrong with me. I was having a meltdown and I didn't even know why.

Jake turned and looked at Laurel. "So how was softball practice?" he asked.

"Oh, shut up," Laurel said.

Jake looked at me, and when he saw the puzzled expression on my face, said with a laugh, "Laurel's not really on the team. She just pretends."

"So my asshole stepmom will leave me alone," Laurel said.

"Oh," I said.

"It's like, she won't let me even go out at all unless she thinks I'm at practice. So I went the first week, got the clothes, and now I just put them on after school so I'm wearing them when I go home."

It wasn't anything I could ever see myself doing, but it still seemed pretty smart. I would have been too afraid that someone would see me and then want me to play catch or something. They'd see how horrible I was at throwing the ball and they'd know I was a total faker, and then they'd call Mom and explain the whole thing, and it would all be downhill from there.

I was sitting there digesting Laurel's explanation when suddenly I felt a sharp prick in the back of my neck.

"Hey!" I cried.

When I turned around, I saw Kari looking at something pinched between her finger and her thumb. "You had a weird hair on your neck," she said.

"You can't just pull people's hair!"

She looked at me, her eyes dead. "Sorry," she said, but she didn't sound sorry. If anything, she sounded pleased.

I turned around, massaging my neck. I was a little afraid to lean all the way back, since she might strike again. Jake leaned over, whispering so only I could hear him.

36

"I think she likes you," he said.

"What?"

He winked at me and went back to driving. I knew there was a strong possibility Jake was just messing with me, but then he might have been telling the truth, and if so, I had something new to worry about. Back then, I was as clueless about girls as I was about everything else in my life. Other boys seemed to have no trouble asking them out on a date, making out in parked cars, but I had never even held hands with a girl.

"Hey!" Laurel cried, making me jump. "It's Paul Schooner!"

I followed where she was pointing—it was hard not to, since her arm was brushing my cheek—and saw two high school kids in a jacked-up black Camaro in the Elks Lodge parking lot. The one driving had slicked black hair and black sunglasses, and he wore a black leather jacket with no shirt underneath. The one in the passenger seat was bigger and pudgier, with only a stubble of brown hair on his sweaty scalp. He had the thickest, fuzziest uni-brow I had ever seen, like a giant black caterpillar.

Laurel laughed and waved, then changed her wave into giving him the bird. The two guys glared at her.

"Prick," Laurel said.

"Who is he?" Jake said.

"My old boyfriend."

We heard a screech of tires. I glanced around and saw the Camaro peeling out of the parking lot. Jake glanced casually in the rearview mirror, smirked, and went right on merrily driving at barely twenty miles an hour. We were on a two-lane road, one lane each way, but the Camaro still pulled alongside of us. The guy driving leaned over his pudgy friend and shouted through the passenger window.

"Who the hell are you?" he said.

"Get out of here, Paul!" Laurel said.

"Shut up, bitch!" Paul shot back. "I'm not talking to you!"

Jake looked at him. "Don't talk to her that way."

He said it without raising his voice, but it still came across crystal clear. It also seemed to surprise Paul, who stared at Jake with his mouth open, before recovering his cool guy act.

"Oooooh," Paul said. "Laurel your girl now, huh? You know she's a total ho, right?"

"I told you not to talk to her that way."

"What, call her a ho? How about *slut*? You like that one better?"

"Paul!" Laurel cried. "You're such a loser!"

A gray van started to pull out from the parking lot of a mini-mart ahead of us, then screeched to a halt just before it banged into the Camaro. Laurel screamed and the guy in the van laid on his horn. I may have screamed a little, too. Thankfully, it was lost in all the horn blaring and Laurel screaming. Paul just laughed. Mr. Uni-brow looked a little more worried. We made eye contact, and it was like we shared a connection. I could see it in his eyes: We both knew how it felt to be prisoners in a situation we didn't create.

"Why don't you go jerk off or something," Jake said.

"Dude, you're so going to regret saying that."

Jake smirked. "Oh, is that a threat?"

"It's a fact," Paul said. "You wanna race?"

"Where?"

"To the end of this road, right where it curves."

Jake looked down the road. He was obviously considering it.

"Don't," I said. "It's not worth it."

"Aw," Jake said, "it's just a little fun."

"Jake, I really don't want to die."

Paul started making chicken-clucking sounds. "I knew you wouldn't do it! Total pussies!"

Slowly, Jake turned and looked at Paul. Even though I couldn't see his face, I knew he was going to do it. I hadn't been around Jake in a long time, but I knew it the same way I had known he was going to dump his milk on Francine Washburn's head back in the fourth grade, when she had told him that he smelled like a can of worms. Jake had a line you couldn't cross, and if you did, he wasn't going to back down.

"Ready?" Jake said.

"Oh yeah, baby," Paul said.

"Jake—" I began.

But it was too late. Jake slammed on the accelerator and the Mustang roared. The car charged ahead, whipping us back in our seats. I heard the screech of the Camaro's tires, but I was too scared out of my mind to turn and look.

Jake shifted through the gears, but he obviously wasn't as used to the Mustang as Paul was to his Camaro, because Paul pulled even with us after just a little while, grinning like a guy in a toothpaste commercial. Then both cars were in fifth gear, and each car was going faster—sixty, seventy—the old downtown changing to a mixture of run-down houses and run-down businesses, then just run-down houses—chipping paint and junk-filled driveways, trees and driveways a blur of green and gray. Laurel was yelling—from excitement or fear, I didn't know. Kari didn't make a sound. I braced myself against the dashboard. *"Jaaaaaaaaaaaaaaaake!"* I cried, the wind swallowing my voice.

Jake had a steely-eyed look, and he was concentrating on the road ahead. The cars were even, the Camaro getting a little ahead, then the Mustang. We were blocking both lanes of traffic, and I kept waiting for a car to pull out of one of the side streets or driveways. I could now see the bend in the road too, and there was a cluster of pine trees on either side of the road down there, making it impossible to see if a car was coming. The Camaro was edging ahead.

"Ha-ha!" Paul yelled. "Suck-errrrrr!"

Then a car did round the bend ahead and I cried out in surprise. It wasn't just any car either. It was a police car—a white one with blue stripes, the sirens blaring on right away.

Both drivers slammed on their brakes. The Camaro took a hard left onto a side street. I was hoping Jake would just stop and get the whole thing over with—the handcuffs, the time behind bars, the tearful call to our parents—but I should have known better. He screeched to the right, onto a narrow road into a residential neighborhood, just missing a big rusty motorhome. Laurel screamed. I screamed. Jake laughed. Kari didn't make a peep.

"What're you doing?" I cried. "You can't get away from the police!"

"He'll probably follow the other guy."

40

The police car, now two blocks back, screeched around the corner and barreled after us. I stared at Jake.

"Okay, maybe not," he said.

I was going to say something else, but he jerked the wheel to the left and screeched around another corner. A cat, sunning itself in the middle of the road on a manhole, darted out of the way just in time. One-story houses and parked cars blurred past. He jerked around another corner and another. I heard the police siren gaining on us.

"You're going to kill someone!" I shouted.

"You're right," he said.

He screeched the car to a halt right in the middle of the road and was out of the car before I could even take a breath.

"Run for it!" he said.

"What?"

"Run! Run!"

He was already sprinting away. Laurel and Kari quickly followed. I sat there like a lump of flesh, trying to get air into my lungs, not sure what to do. Running might make it worse. But if I didn't run, I would be the only one left to suffer the consequences. The police siren rounded onto the street, and it was as if I'd been jabbed with an electric cattle prod, because I jumped out of the car and started after Jake. Then I remembered I'd left the backpack in the Mustang. I turned. The police car was halfway down the street, lights flashing, close enough that I could see the cop inside—a beefy guy with a hamster-size brown mustache.

I hesitated. Dad's portrait was in the backpack.

"What are you doing?" Jake shouted at me from down the road.

I couldn't leave the backpack. I ran back for it, lunging inside and pulling it out. The cop car screeched to a halt next to the Mustang.

"Stop right there!" the cop shouted.

But I was already running.

chapter five

In my mind, I saw the whole thing playing out like some episode from *Cops*. I saw myself running from the scene of the crime, eyes crazed. Maybe I was shirtless. I knew I wouldn't look good without a shirt, kind of like how one of those hairless cats looks, but the criminals never seemed to be wearing shirts on those shows. I saw the policeman pulling out his gun. I heard gunshots—*bam! bam! bam!*—three in a row, each one finding its target in my legs. I saw myself going down in a heap. I heard the deep-voiced narrator speaking as I lay writhing on the ground, the camera focusing on my blood pooling on the sidewalk: "Charles Hill had a bright future ahead of him, but it all ended on one tragic afternoon when he was in the wrong place at the wrong time."

"You, kid!" the policeman shouted behind me. "Hold it!"

But I didn't stop. Lucky for me, there were no gunshots. Jake and the two girls had already rounded the corner and I ran after them as fast as my puny legs would take me, my backpack slung over my shoulder feeling like it was full of bricks. I heard the police car's engine roar, and glancing back, saw the car swerve around the Mustang and head right for me.

Why was I running? It made no sense. I was a good kid. I was not a lawbreaker. I did not want to die.

I reached the corner, gasping already, and saw the two girls take a hard left after a big ugly green bush. The policeman turned the corner right after I did, tires screeching, and pulled right along-side of me. I didn't dare look at him. Dogs were barking; an old lady glared at me from her kitchen window; a Hispanic man wearing a baseball cap stopped pushing his lawn mower and stared. I reached the bush and banked left, finding a narrow sidewalk path that connected two streets, the backyard fences on either side making it seem like a tunnel. Jake was halfway down, the girls ahead of him, and he was madly waving me on.

Behind me, the cop car screeched to a halt. The door opened and slammed shut. I heard heavy booted footsteps on the pavement.

"Stop!" the guy shouted again. You'd think by now he would have realized that the whole shouting thing wasn't working for him.

When I reached Jake, he took off across the street. We were in a cul-de-sac, both sides of the street lined with junky cars, and I saw the girls climbing over a wooden fence of a yellow house. Jake scaled it like a pole vaulter on his gold-medal run. Me, I barely managed to get my leg and one arm up, struggling to get all the way over the top.

Finally, I fell to the other side, onto a prickly hedge of junipers. I was up in a hurry. Jake was already climbing a fence on the far side. I got to it and managed to get over and down into another backyard before I heard the policeman behind me. This lawn was as immaculate as a golf course, shaped like an hourglass.

"This way!"

I turned, and there was Jake, half out of a tall hedge. He ducked inside, and I plunged after him, branches whipping my sweaty face. We emerged into another backyard, the house big, green, and boxy like an army barrack. We rushed around the corner and there were the girls, breathing hard, faces pink. Laurel led us behind a huge woodpile, the rest of us following. It was shadowy and damp, and there were dozens of cigarette butts in the dirt. It smelled like rotting wood and mold.

"What now?" I said.

Laurel put her fingers to her lips. She listened for a moment, and when she didn't hear anything, leaned in close and whispered.

"I live a few houses from here," she said. "When the cop's gone, we'll go there."

"You been here before?" Jake asked.

"Oh yeah, lots of times." She smiled. "This is Paul's house. You know, the guy with the Camaro. We used to hang out behind the wood here and make out."

I looked at her, waiting for the punch line. But she was serious. So if the cop didn't get us, her ex-boyfriend would show up and want to fight. Nice.

The neighborhood dogs barked in surround sound, and we heard the rattle of a chain-link fence a couple of houses over, but the cop didn't find us. Neither did Camaro Paul. We waited another minute or so, then Laurel peered into the next backyard. She motioned for us to go, and we climbed into the branches of an apple tree and down into a backyard that was all bark dust, dirt, and fallen rotting apples.

Creeping along, crouched like a platoon on a patrol, we crossed that yard, and two more after it, then went into the backyard of a big two-story white house with a covered porch that made me think of the house from *The Waltons*. I'm not sure if I'd ever seen an episode of *The Waltons*, but it's the house I imagined people like the Waltons would live in. Clean-cut, nice people. Not people like Laurel, who smoked and kissed jerks behind woodpiles.

We stood on the side of the house, with a view of the backyard, a huge pine tree above us blotting out the sky. Laurel closed the wooden gate, holding the latch so it didn't make a sound.

"Stay here," she whispered. "My stepmom might be home."

She went around the corner. Kari stood off to the side, picking something out of her fingernails with a pine needle. My legs felt like jelly. My shirt was soaked with sweat. I wondered how I was going to get out of this mess without getting into any more trouble.

When I'd gotten my breath back, I said, "They're going to find out it's us, you know."

"Nah," Jake said.

"They will. They're going to trace the license plate, then they'll call Harkin and he'll tell them we stole it."

He shrugged. "So what's in the bag?"

"Huh?"

"Your backpack. What's so important that you had to go back for it?"

"Uh . . . well, it's got like all my information in it. They'd know it was me for sure if I left it back there."

He shook his head. "I saw the look you had. There's something important in there you didn't want to leave."

I didn't want to tell him about Dad's portrait. I knew he'd never understand and that he'd probably just make fun of me. Laurel came around the corner, saving me from having to say anything.

"She's gone," she said. "My brother said she went to the store."

"Tim's here?" Jake said.

"No, Tim's at soccer practice. He's really into that sports stuff. I mean my brother Gabe. I don't think you've met him—lives in Bend. Just here for the day, I think. Don't worry, he's cool. Smokes too much pot, but cool."

We followed her onto the deck and through the sliding glass doors into the house. I was still worried that the cops might show up at any minute. We entered a family room with dark-paneled walls, leather furniture, and a big TV/stereo setup. There was a green felt poker table in the corner and pictures of poker-playing bulldogs on the walls. The room was cool and had the air-conditioned staleness of a house that didn't get a lot of fresh air.

I wasn't paying attention to where Jake was, and suddenly my backpack was jerked off my shoulder. I lunged for it, but he pranced away with it above his head.

"Got it!" He laughed.

"Give that back!"

"Not until I see what's inside."

"Jake—"

"More love notes to Tessa Boone?"

"It's nothing like that! Give it to me!"

The girls just stood and watched. Laurel giggled. Somehow Jake managed to keep his body between me and the backpack, his back like a wall, despite how hard I tried to get around him. I heard him unzip it.

"No!" I protested.

"Let's see here," he said, dropping some books on the floor, "boring school stuff, some notebooks with notes—"

"Jake!"

"—a wadded-up paper sack with . . . *ewww*, broccoli and cauliflower—"

"Stop!"

"—some nerdy sci-fi paperbacks, a cheap Swiss army knife, a . . . compass? Okay, weird. And . . ." He trailed off.

Finally, I managed to get past his blockade, and I saw that he was looking at my drawing notebook. Not only that, but he had it open and he was looking at the portrait of Dad. I snatched it away from him, cradling it against my chest. He looked at me. All the joking was gone, and he looked at me in a totally different way. He looked impressed.

"You drew that, man?" he said.

I shrugged.

"It's really good. Who is it?"

"Nobody." I felt a warmth in my cheeks.

"Let me see it!" Laurel said.

"No," I said.

"Aww, come on!"

"It's not any good."

Jake shook his head. "Dude, you're selling yourself short. That's a totally frickin' awesome drawing."

Laurel put her hands on the pad and tugged at it. I put up a little resistance, but not really that much, and she took it away from me. The truth was, I wanted her to like it. I wanted it to be true, what Jake said, but I was afraid he was just full of it and she would

48

say something like, "Oh, that's nice," in that fake way that people use when they can't be bothered to form an opinion either way.

But she didn't say it. She didn't say anything for a long time. She just looked at it, her eyes wide.

"Wow," she said finally.

"I told you it's not good," I said.

"Man, didn't you hear her?" Jake said. "She thinks it's awesome."

"People'd pay money for drawings like this," she said.

"I knew you always kind of doodled," Jake said, "but I didn't know you were this good. Who's the guy?"

"I told you, nobody."

"Come on, tell me. Is it your dad or something?"

He said it with a laugh. I looked at him, and I knew I couldn't hide my surprise that he'd guessed it straight off.

"That's it!" he said.

I shrugged.

"Wow, man. That's cool. Your dad, he lives like on the other side of the country, though, right?"

"Kind of," I said. "He lives in Denver."

"Are you going to mail it to him?"

"I don't know."

"You should."

"He wouldn't like it anyway."

"I bet he would!" Laurel said. "I bet he'd love it!"

"You should take it to him yourself personally," Kari said.

She hadn't spoken in so long, I'd forgotten she was even in the room. She was actually looking at me, and it was unnerving, the

49

way she stared. Her face was frozen, not even her hair moving; it made her look like one of those Russian dolls.

The silence was getting awkward. I took the pad from Laurel, closed it, and stuck it into my backpack. Then I picked the things Jake had dropped off the floor.

"Hey," Laurel said, tugging Jake on the arm. "You want to come to my room for a while? I . . . got some new songs on my iPod."

Jake smiled. "Sure, babe," he said.

"We'll be back in a little while," Laurel said, and took Jake's hand and led him out of the room.

I heard her giggling in the hallway. Then a door shut. I stood next to Kari. She was still staring at me. I tried not to stare back, but I couldn't take the drilling of her eyes for long.

"What?" I said.

"You're kinda cute," she said.

There was a fist-size lump in my throat, and I swallowed it away.

"Oh," I said.

"I mean, kinda bruised and all. But cute."

"Okay. Thanks."

"You wanna make out?"

"Um . . . no. No, that's okay. Thanks."

"You can even touch my boobs if you want."

I was having a hard time meeting her eyes, but I looked at her to see if she was joking, and she didn't seem to be joking. It was hard to tell, really, with Kari, but she definitely seemed to be serious. My heart was pounding, and I felt sweat on the back of my neck. It was like I'd been trying to bang down a door to a locked room all my life and now suddenly someone had just opened it for me and invited me inside.

"Oh," I said. "Oh wow. Thanks . . . I, uh. . . no."

I couldn't believe what I was saying. This girl had *actually asked me to touch her boobs,* and here I was saying no. She shrugged, doing her best to look like she didn't care, but there was something about her eyes that made me think I'd hurt her. I didn't want her to think I'd rejected her. It wasn't about her. I didn't know what it was about, but I knew it wasn't her. She was definitely pretty, in a strange sort of way. If I was in the mood to touch a girl's boobs, she'd be the first on the list. I thought about saying this, but then decided it probably wouldn't come out right.

"I could draw you," I offered, and immediately regretted saying it.

She looked at me again, her eyes brimming. "Really?"

"Um, sure. Only if you want. You don't have to do it. I mean, it wouldn't be any good."

"I want to."

"Okay."

"Do you want me naked?"

I didn't think I'd heard her right. "Huh?"

"Naked. I know artists like to draw nudes."

"Um . . . no. No, that's okay. You can wear your clothes."

"I don't mind."

"No, really, it's okay."

"Okay. If you're sure."

"I'm sure, I'm sure."

"Are you okay?"

"Huh?"

"Your face. It's all red."

I was sweating so much that it was running into my eyes. Now she was a big white-and-black blur. I knew I had the unfortunate habit of turning into a tomato when I was embarrassed. It was one of the things that I hated about me. There were lots of things I hated about me, but that was right at the top of the list.

"Yeah, it's a little hot in here is all," I said.

"Okay. Where?"

"Huh?"

"Where do you want to draw me?"

"Well, here. In the room. Oh, right, you mean, where in the room. Okay. How about on the couch there. Just sitting there on the corner. I'll—I'll get my drawing pencils. Go ahead. Um. Sit down."

She went to the couch, perching on the edge. I watched her for a moment, then remembered I needed to get my drawing pencils. The room felt like it was rocking back and forth, like we were in the hull of a ship. If I wasn't careful, I'd fall down. I riffled through the bag, found the pencils, then sat on the love seat across from her. She was staring at me blankly. I smiled weakly. She went on staring. I opened my drawing pad to a new page and got to work, starting with her general outline and then filling in her details.

The whole thing was surreal. In the last few hours, I'd been beaten up in a fight, stolen the principal's car, escaped from the police, been asked to make out by a girl, and now here I was, sitting in some strange house drawing a girl who'd offered to pose naked. It wasn't me. The real me was back in Rexton, sitting in my room, feeling sore from Leo's beating, wondering how I was going to make it through another day of high school. And yet, as much as I wanted to go home, there was part of me that was kind of enjoying it all, weird as that was. It was like trying on a new jacket that you thought you'd hate, but once you'd put it on, you wanted to wear it a little while longer. You still weren't sure you liked it, but it was different, and different wasn't bad.

· chapter
SIX

There is this place I go when I'm deep into a drawing, this place inside my mind where time doesn't even pass. It passes on the outside world, but it doesn't pass for me. It's a nice place, a place where I'm alone and at peace, and for once in my life, totally free from all the doubting and worrying and second-guessing. It was the reason I liked drawing so much. Back then, it wasn't so much about the drawing itself. It was about going to that place and staying there as long as I could.

It seemed like I'd only been drawing a minute, but then I felt someone nudge me on the shoulder. I blinked a few times and looked up to see Jake smiling down at me. His blond hair looked tousled, and his T-shirt was rumpled. The light in the room had waned, the air dusky. I had a crick in my neck.

"You with us, space cadet?" he said.

Laurel stood in the doorway, smiling and dopey-eyed. Her red hair, once pulled back in a ponytail, was loose and looked like she'd just run a balloon over it, loose hairs sticking out with static in every direction. She wore a different shirt, a black Spider-Man tank top that was a bit too small. I had a good idea what she and Jake had been doing. Well, not *exactly*, since all that stuff was still a mystery to me, but an idea, anyway.

There was also another guy standing next to her, a real skinny dude with short purple spiked hair and pink-tinted glasses. His goatee was purple too. I glanced at the couch, and Kari was still in the same position, as good as a statue.

"Nice," Jake said, nodding at the drawing.

"Are you finished?" Kari asked.

Laurel and the new guy came around to Jake's side to examine the drawing. Laurel whistled her approval. I wasn't sure I was finished, but then Kari got up and came around to look. She stared a long time and didn't say a word. I figured she was going to laugh or call it crap, which I figured it was, but then she did something I didn't expect. She started crying.

"Oh man, I'm sorry," I said. "I'll rip it up."

She sniffled. "You made me look beautiful."

"Huh?"

"Can I have it?"

Wordlessly, I tore out the drawing and handed it to her. I didn't even think twice about it. I never gave my pictures to anyone, but there was no way I could say no to her after she had cried. She took it over to the couch and sat down, staring at the picture. She was smiling, the first time I'd seen her smile, and she looked almost like a different person when she did. We all watched her for a moment, as if waiting for her to do something else amazing, but she just went on staring at it.

It was a feeling I'd never had before, watching somebody cry over something I'd drawn. I wanted to do it again. Maybe not make somebody cry, that would be kind of twisted, but make them feel *something*. Anything. All at once I understood why people still became artists when everybody knew, like my dad had told me lots of times when I was little, that artists always ended up living in their parents' basements.

"Well," Jake said, "at least now we know how you can get girls."

"Excuse me, dudes," the guy with the purple hair said. "I don't mean to intrude on your situation, but if you want to come with me, I'd like to know."

"Go with him?" I said.

Jake and Laurel exchanged glances.

"Yeah," Jake said, "that's something we wanted to talk to you about. Gabe said we could hitch a ride with him in his van. We just have to chip in for gas."

"Hitch a ride where?" I said.

"To Bend."

"Bend!"

Jake nodded. "Yeah, for starters. Then maybe hitch a ride from there. Or hop a bus. He says there's a Greyhound station in Bend."

This wasn't making any sense to me. Bend was over a two-hour drive away, up over the Cascade mountains. I'd been there once as a kid, on a disastrous ski trip that ended up with me breaking my ankle, and I hadn't been there since. "What do you mean, 'from there'? What are you talking about?"

He hesitated. "I'm talking about delivering that picture of yours in person."

"What?"

Laurel chimed in, "To your dad!"

"My dad! He lives in Colorado! That's like over a thousand miles away from Oregon!"

Jake shrugged. "So it'll take a while to get there. Laurel and I got to talking about it, and I think it makes sense. I think it's something you should do. And I'll help."

The utter insanity of the idea was hard for me to even comprehend, and Jake was talking about it as if it was just going to the movies for the afternoon. "I can't go to Denver!"

"Why not? It'd be fun."

"Fun!"

"Yeah. A road trip. Just the two of us."

I was waiting for him to laugh, to tell me he was joking, but he looked completely serious. "Jake," I blurted, "we can't go to Denver!"

"Why?"

"Why? Because, because we're high school kids, that's why! Because we don't have any money! Because I've never even been to my dad's house! Because—because—because it's stupid and insane!"

He smiled. "You want to do it, I can tell."

"You're insane!"

"And I've got money." He reached into the pocket of his jean jacket and pulled out a money clip full of a big wad of cash.

"Where'd you get that?" I said.

"From my piggy bank," he said.

"I'm serious!"

"I am too. I've been saving for a while. It's over five hundred dollars."

"We still can't go!"

"Aw," he said, "come on. I know it seems nuts, but that's why it's so cool. Imagine the look on your dad's face when you give him that picture. Just imagine. Priceless, baby. Totally priceless. And we'll have a lot of fun getting there."

I shook my head. "Don't you think our parents will miss us?"

"Who cares? We're doing this for us, not them."

"They'd send the police after us."

He laughed. "Maybe your mom would."

"Hey dudes," Gabe said, "this is all very interesting and whatnot, but perhaps your commitment to this plan of action is not yet one hundred percent. I'm going to leave you to your discussions and return to packing." He actually talked like that. I'd never heard a person who sounded just like him, like a cross between a surfer and a professor.

"We're going," Jake said firmly.

"No way," I said.

"Aw, come on, man. Do it! Take a risk. Don't be such a pussy."

After everything I'd been through, I was starting to feel like maybe I wasn't such a wimp, so his insult stung. "Screw you," I said. I grabbed my bag and headed for the door.

"Charlie—"

"I'm going home."

I went out the screen door and down the deck steps to the grass, heading for the gate. The air had cooled since I was last outside, the sun low in the sky. The swings swayed slightly in the breeze. I didn't care if the cops were still out there looking for me. I was going home.

"Charlie," Jake called to me.

"Leave me alone," I said.

"What, are you going to walk home?"

"If I have to!"

"Come on, Charlie—"

I turned and faced him. "Leave me alone!"

He raised his hands, caught off guard by my anger. The thing was, I was scared, and it wasn't because I *didn't* want to go. It was because I actually did. Crazy as it was, I wanted to go to Denver and find my dad and give him the portrait. I knew I would probably end up in even worse trouble than I was now, that it was stupid and impulsive and bound to fail on every single level, but I still wanted to go. The only thing waiting for me at home was Mom, and her soon-to-be-husband, Rick, and Leo's fists, and the whole school knowing about Tessa Boone, and a thousand other things that would make my sucky life even suckier when I got back to it. Going on a spontaneous road trip—it scared me out of my mind, but it was different. And I really wanted something different. I'd been wanting something different my whole life.

I knew that if I stayed there any longer, I might just do something crazy like say yes, and I couldn't let that happen.

"I'll see you back at school," I said, and left through the gate.

Every couple of blocks, I glanced over my shoulder to see if Jake was following, but he wasn't. I didn't see any cops, just some kids riding bikes and a father and son playing catch. I had only a vague sense of which way was home, but I figured if I kept ending up on bigger and longer streets, eventually I'd end up someplace where

59

I could decide which direction I needed to go. I also figured, if it came to it, I could just ask to borrow somebody's phone and call Mom and ask her to come get me.

Go to Colorado. Give the picture to Dad.

That's what a little voice inside my head was saying. I tried to ignore it. Dad wouldn't want to see me. Even if he did, there was no way we could get there on our own, even if Jake *did* have five hundred dollars. And even if we did manage to get there, it would take days, maybe weeks, and I couldn't miss that much school. Mom would go crazy with worry.

But I still wanted to do it.

It was like the note I had written to Tessa Boone. I didn't want to admit it to Jake, but I did write it. I had written it even knowing that she was Leo Gonzalez's girlfriend. I had written it knowing that if it ever got to her, she would certainly give it to Leo. I'd been thinking about her for months, imagining her naked and giving me massages and that sort of thing, and the more I told myself that she was taken, that Leo would kill me, the more I wanted to write her a note. It was the craziest thing. So I wrote it. I wrote it and then I carried it around in my notebook for weeks, planning all the different ways I might give it to her.

The only strange part was, I didn't remember actually giving it to her. I may have dreamed it, but I didn't actually remember doing it for real. That's what scared me. It scared me that I might do the same thing here, that I might blank out for a while like I obviously had with the note and agree to get into the van and go to Denver without even realizing I was doing it.

Forget about the Ivy League. It wouldn't be long before somebody checked me into a mental institution.

I'd been walking for about ten minutes when I heard an obnoxious motor behind me, and I turned and saw an old Volkswagen van that was a motley green, as if covered with seaweed. It hadn't been painted that way deliberately; it was just the uneven way the paint had chipped and faded over time. Sitting in the driver's seat was Gabe, and next to him in the passenger's seat was Jake. They pulled up beside me, the motor hacking and sputtering like an old guy with emphysema. The door slid open and Jake leaned out. He held a piece of paper in his hand.

"Get in," he said.

"I already told you—"

"I know what you said. But if you don't do it, I'm going to do it for you."

"What are you talking about?"

He turned the paper around. It was Dad's portrait. I couldn't believe it. I reached for it, and he jerked it away.

"Uh-unn," he said. "You gotta come with us to have it."

"How'd you get that?" I said.

"My secret," he said.

"You took it out of my bag when I was drawing!"

"Maybe."

"I don't believe this. Give it to me."

"Nope. If you don't come, I'm going to give it to your dad for you."

"I don't believe this," I said again.

"Come on, Charlie. Let's do it. It'll be fun. An adventure."

"Why does it matter so much to you?"

He shrugged. "Because I want to see his face. I want to see his face when you give it to him."

He said it as if he hadn't put any thought into it, but I realized, right when he said it, it was exactly what I wanted too. It wasn't so much about giving Dad the picture as seeing his face when I gave it to him. I wasn't sure why exactly, but it seemed very important. I also knew that if I didn't get into the van that very moment, I'd never give it to him. I would never be brave enough to do it myself, even if I was standing right across from him, and I would certainly never mail it. If I didn't go, I was pretty sure it would gnaw at me for the rest of my life.

The problem was, if I went, I knew I might regret that for the rest of my life too. There might have still been a way to get my life back on track, my quiet little highway to a good college and eventually to medical school. That's what I wanted, wasn't it? Like Mr. Harkin had said, I wanted to be a doctor just like Dad.

Didn't I?

So there I was, standing on the street corner in a city I didn't live in, thinking about getting into a van driven by some quasi-hippie guy I'd just met, wondering if I should go on a cross-country road trip with a guy I hadn't been friends with since the fourth grade, a guy that was by all accounts not really right in the head. Charlie, the Human Squid, bruised and confused, stealer of cars and writer of secret love notes, Charlie who was about to do something that could possibly turn out to be the stupidest thing he'd ever done in his life. Or the best. Only time would tell.

"Okay," I said, and I got into the van.

chapter seven

The floor of the van was covered with the brightest orange shag carpeting I'd ever seen. It was like walking on an orange peel. The walls were decorated with faded black-and-white photocopies of wizened Asian men with long beards, most of them smoking long pipes. Colorful beads separated the driver's area from the rest of the van, and there were pastel-colored paper wind chimes hanging in the rear, twirling endlessly. Instead of seats, there was a plaid couch and a purple beanbag. The van smelled so strongly of pine—from the little green tree air freshener hanging from the rearview mirror—that I had a headache immediately.

Gabe had barely put the van in gear and I was already having second thoughts. What was I doing? I was going to throw my life away being stupid. But then we were moving, and I told myself to just calm down, that it would all work out for the best, even if I didn't know how yet. I could always find a way home from Bend. So I wasn't committing to a long road trip, not yet—just one evening. One evening couldn't ruin my life. And it was fun. I kept repeating that to myself. You're having fun. You can always back out later. If nothing else, this will be a great story you can tell girls to impress them, which is a lot better than telling them you have every single issue of the original *Transformers* comic book series.

Jake and I sat next to each other on the couch. I looked for seat belts, going so far as to dig under cushions.

"Dude, relax," Jake said.

"I just—I don't want to die, you know," I said.

"You won't die. Come on, it's not . . ."

He trailed off, and I saw why. We were passing Mr. Harkin's Mustang, still parked in the center of the street where Jake had left it, and that wasn't all: Mr. Harkin himself stood next to the car, looking inside it, and there were two policemen on the other side watching him. As the van rumbled past, they all looked at us.

Both Jake and I had the same reaction. We ducked out of sight.

Gabe glanced back, raising his eyebrows. His pink glasses had darkened to crimson from the glare of the low sun. "You gentlemen in any trouble with the police?" he said, sounding like an inspector from an Agatha Christie novel. He had to speak loudly to be heard over the grinding roar of the engine.

"Nah," Jake said. "We're just stretching our legs."

It was obvious Gabe didn't believe it, but he shrugged and returned his attention to the road. Since we heard no sirens and saw no police cars tailing us, we moved back to the couch.

"You dudes really venturing all the way to the great state of Colorado?" Gabe asked.

"Yep," Jake said.

"Fabulous. I've been to Colorado."

We waited for him to say something more, but he didn't. He clicked on the radio. It was some sixties band singing about love, which really didn't narrow it down, I know, but I didn't know much about sixties music. Actually, I didn't really know much about music at all, except that I should never admit I liked Britney Spears around anyone my age. Probably not around anyone of any age, though I'd never tested it. When you've been laughed at by an entire classroom because of your choice in music, you don't tend to speak about it again.

The van passed through the neighborhoods and the small Grantville downtown, and after passing fields with grazing goats, cows, and llamas, we were back on Highway 47, headed east. The sky was turning a hazy dark blue, and the few streaks of clouds looked liked they'd been slapped up there by a quick dash from a paintbrush.

"It's going to be night soon," I said.

"Yeah," Jake says, "that usually happens."

"I don't have a toothbrush."

"What a crisis."

I looked at him. "You're making fun of me."

"Yep." He laughed and punched me lightly on the shoulder. "Come on, man, we're on the road! Don't worry about small stuff. We'll figure it out."

"Okay," I said, still wondering what I was going to do without my toothbrush.

"Tell me something," he said.

"Yeah."

"Did you write that note?"

"Huh?"

"The one to Tessa Boone."

I thought about what to say, then decided, what the heck. I'd already abandoned reason back on the sidewalk in Grantville. "Yeah, I did."

"Wow. Really?"

"Yeah."

"Put it in her locker and everything?"

I hesitated. I still didn't remember doing that part, but I didn't want him to think I was any crazier than I already seemed. "Yep. Stupid, huh?"

He turned and watched the passing landscape. We were beyond the reaches of the cities outlying Rexton now, passing through rugged ranchland, a few tall pine trees here and there lining the road as we approached the foothills of the Cascade mountains. The flat highway had turned into a gradual rise.

"Why her?" he said finally.

"Huh?"

He looked at me, squinting as if he was trying to see the hidden image in one of those pictures with all the colored dots. "I mean, was it just her looks? She's pretty hot, I guess. But she seems so . . . I don't know, *empty*. It's one thing if you were just hanging out with her and getting some action, but writing a love note . . ."

"It was more than just looks," I said defensively.

"Oh yeah? What is it you like about her?"

"Well, she's . . . well, for starters, she's . . ."

I struggled to come up with a single thing about her I liked that wouldn't seem shallow. She had a great smile. She looked good in her cheerleader outfit. Somebody on the street might mistake her for Pamela Anderson's little sister. None of that would sound good. I could say she was nice, I guess, but it was more that she wasn't awful to me, unlike a lot of other girls. But that didn't mean she was treating me any different than she treated lots of other geeky guys.

"It's hard picking out one thing," I said.

"That's bull," he said. "She's got big boobs and she's a cheerleader. 'Nuff said."

"No, no, it's more than that. She's—She's made the honor roll. And she's always in the advanced classes."

"Ooooo, honor roll and advanced classes. Who cares? Even if she is the smartest one in school, it's not why you like her."

"Oh yeah?" I said. "You've got it all figured out, huh?"

He nodded smugly. "You like her because you can't have her."

"What? That makes no sense at all."

"It makes perfect sense. You obsess about some girl you can't have. That way you never really have to let a girl you *can* have get close to you. It's classic." He crossed his arms behind his head and leaned back on the couch, his long blond hair fanning out behind him, and I found myself getting angry at his arrogance.

"It's stupid is what it is," I said. "I really liked Tessa a lot."

"*Liked?* As in, you don't anymore? It's over that quick, huh?"

I sighed. "What I meant—"

"You've never gotten laid, have you?"

"What?"

"Come on," he said, "it's okay to admit it. You're a virgin."

I felt the blood rushing to my cheeks, good old tomato face coming out in full force. No way I could bluff my way through this one. He'd see right through me.

"So what if I haven't?" I retorted. "I just haven't met the right girl. Besides, I think it's better to wait until you're married for that sort of thing."

He snorted. "Okay, sure, whatever."

"I do."

"All right, fine. You ever even kissed a girl?"

"Sure, lots of times." I answered quickly, hoping that if I showed no hesitation he'd be more likely to believe me.

"Uh-huh," he said. "Who?"

"Oh, you know, different girlfriends." I was really on thin ice now.

"You've had girlfriends?"

"Sure."

He shook his head. "You're lying."

"Am not."

"Am too."

I leaned forward, yelling at Gabe. "Stop the van! I'm getting out!"

"Don't listen to him!" Jake yelled. "He doesn't mean it!"

Gabe looked at us with a blank expression, then went back to driving.

"I'm not lying," I said quietly.

"Okay, whatever," Jake said. "It's no skin off my back anyway. I just thought you might want to talk about it. I could maybe give you some pointers."

"Oh, and I guess you're all Mr. Experienced and everything, then. Huh?"

He shrugged. "I don't know. I've definitely been with girls. I mean, I don't want to brag or anything, but I just got laid today."

"Right."

"I did, man. You can call Laurel and ask her if you want. She wouldn't be happy I told you, but she wouldn't lie about it."

I thought about the way he and Laurel had looked after Jake had woken me from my drawing-induced coma, and I knew there was a good chance he was telling the truth. I'd heard guys bragging about it sometimes in the bathrooms, talking about stuff like who would go down and who wouldn't, and all that stuff that only vaguely made sense to me, but I never thought most of them really had done it. Maybe I knew deep down a lot of them *were* doing it, but it was easier to pretend they weren't.

In reality, I hated that I'd never been with a girl, but I didn't know what to do about it. When even talking to girls was terrifying, it was hard to imagine putting my lips on a girl, much less doing more. Plus I knew there was something to what he was saying about me obsessing about girls I couldn't have. There had been a few girls who'd shown an interest in me, some girls in my art classes and stuff, but none of them seemed interesting. Now I wondered if I didn't think they were interesting because they were interested in me. In other words, if they were interested in me, that must have meant there was something wrong with them.

Or maybe I was just a snob. Maybe I thought I was better than them. Any way you looked at it, it was bad. And depressing. Just more reasons to hate myself.

"Whatever," I said, looking out the window. There was hardly any light out there now, and the landscape was just one shadow on top of another, like piles of dark laundry in a dark room.

"Look, Chuckster, I'm not trying to embarrass you or anything. I'm just calling it like I see it."

"Yeah, okay."

"I mean . . . Let me ask you something. It might seem kinda weird, but . . . have you ever, you know, jerked off?"

I was shocked by the question. "What?"

"You don't have to say if you don't want to."

"God!"

"It's really no big deal. Most guys whack off. I mean, what do you do if you get one of those hard-ons that won't go away?"

"I'm not talking about this!"

"It's okay if you haven't. It just explains a few things."

"I didn't say that!"

"All right, all right."

We rode in silence, the tires humming over the asphalt underneath us, the engine still loud but no longer sputtering. I couldn't believe he was trying to get me to talk about stuff like sex and whacking off. The thing was, he was right. I hadn't whacked off, and I knew I was missing something big, something a lot of guys were doing by the time they were sixteen, but how do you go about learning what to do? It wasn't like they offered a class in it. It wasn't like they talked about it in Sex Ed., other than to say masturbation was a normal part of sexual awakening, as if that meant anything to me. I got boners all the time, usually when I didn't want them, like when I was about to stand up from my desk in class, and I knew that boners were part of the whole sex thing, but words like *jerking* and *whacking* sounded like you were supposed to hurt yourself, and I wasn't going to do that. As a general rule, I avoided pain.

I once tried to look for some sex books in the public library, but I had gotten nervous when one of the librarians had asked if she could help me find anything. I hadn't even been near the sex books yet. I had been holding a Julia Child cookbook at the time.

"Let me ask you something," I said, deciding to change the subject. "Why do you want to do this?"

"What's that?"

"Go on this trip—you know, to see my dad. Why is it so important to you?"

"I told you, I just want to see his face when you give him that picture."

"Okay," I said. "Why?"

"What?"

"Why do you want to see his face?"

His forehead furrowed. "Why? I don't know. Just 'cause. What's with all the questions?"

"Oh, it's all right for you to ask me lots of questions," I said, "but I can't ask you any?"

"Well, not if they don't make sense."

"They make perfect sense," I said. "I just don't think you're telling me everything. I just think you've got another reason for wanting to do this, and you're not saying."

"Dude, you've got it all wrong. I'm really in it just for the kicks."

"All the way to Denver just for kicks?"

"That's right."

"You're full of it."

"Yeah, okay, whatever," he said, obviously mad that I was pushing this.

I suddenly had an idea I thought might lead somewhere. "What's your dad doing anyway?"

He looked at me, his gaze steady, his face now a stone mask. There was no smirk anywhere to be found.

"My dad?" he said.

"Yeah, what's he doing?"

"My foster dad drives a long-haul truck. I don't see him much."

"I wasn't talking about your foster dad. I was talking about your real dad."

He stared at me, his eyes narrowing. "My dad," he said, with an edge to his voice, "is none of your fucking business."

"Whoa," I said, raising my hands. "It was just a question."

"I don't talk about him," Jake said.

"Okay."

"He's a loser."

"All right," I said. "Let's just drop it."

He returned to looking out the window. I wasn't going to say anything, but I knew I was onto something. There was something definitely going on in his life, something that made him want to get out of town.

"Hey," he said, turning to me, suddenly the cocky, smirking Jake again. "You remember the look on that guy's face in the white convertible when we laid one on him? Remember what happened with his toupee?"

It took me a second to realize he had just shifted back in time to the fourth grade, the first summer we had started lobbing water balloons. One of our first victims had been a middle-aged guy in a white convertible. Jake's bright yellow balloon had not only landed right in the middle of the car, but also right on the guy's thick mop of brown hair—or, what we had *thought* was hair. Turned out the hair was actually a bad toupee and in the explosion of water had splatted on the road behind the car like a squashed beaver. That had also been the first guy to screech to a halt and come charging up our steep driveway looking for us.

We had lots of victims after that, but somehow they had never quite measured up to Mr. Toupee. We had repeated the story to each other lots of times, and each time the details changed, his hair getting bigger, his face wetter, his growling threats more menacing.

"Yeah," I said, smiling.

Jake slapped his knee. "That was the best."

"It was pretty funny."

"That was where we got our name, too."

I stared him blankly.

"You don't remember?" he said, and touched his heart as if I had wounded him. He did it in a joking way, but he had a look on his face like me forgetting had actually hurt him a little. "I can't believe you forgot our name."

"Name?" I said, and then right away it came to me. "Water Balloon Boys. We called ourselves the Water Balloon Boys."

"That's right!" he cried, and laughed so loud that Gabe turned and looked at us.

I couldn't remember who had come up with it, but it was a

name we'd used all the way up until the whole Game Boy incident. We'd even made secret cards with our names and *Water Balloon Boys* written on the back, but only in invisible ink that would show up with the black lights we had bought at the local magic shop. We were a famous outlaw gang, and there were WANTED posters for us all over the world. We'd sworn a bond to each other, an oath to be there when it mattered, when the chips were down.

I looked at him, thinking about asking him if he still had his card, but that might lead to the Game Boy incident, and I wasn't ready to go there. He made eye contact with me for a few seconds, and he must have sensed how uneasy I was, because he got up and went to the front, plopping down in the passenger seat and making small talk with Gabe.

But I had seen something else on his face.

I had seen how important being the Water Balloon Boys was to him.

I had seen the face of the kid who had knelt next to me in that pine tree years ago, juicy water balloon in hand, eyes widening at the sound of an approaching car. It was the face of a kid living in a moment of pure happiness, a moment when there was no past and no future, only the great and glorious present that both of us had hoped would go on forever and ever without end. Somewhere in the passing years, I had left that moment behind me, but I realized Jake hadn't. He was still there.

chapter eight

I didn't remember falling asleep, but the next thing I knew, Jake was shaking my shoulder, telling me we were there. I rubbed my eyes, blinking out into darkness, catching a whiff of the night breeze. It took me a moment to remember where *there* was.

"Bend?" I said groggily. I had slept with my head on the side of the couch, and now my neck was sore.

I smelled pine, but it could have just been the air freshener. I wondered if everything would smell like pine now. The van's side door was open and Gabe was grabbing his duffle bag and hefting it onto his shoulder. Jake stood over me, his face shrouded in darkness.

"Yep," Jake said. "I think you fell asleep somewhere on the pass. I tried talking to you a few times, but you were really conked out."

"What time is it?"

"I don't know. I think it's around eight o'clock. Maybe nine."

"That's it?" It felt later.

"Yeah, I know," he said. "Long day. And hey, it's not over yet. Gabe says it looks like his roommates are having a party."

Still feeling disoriented, I followed Jake out of the van, keeping my backpack with me. My sneakers crunched on gravel and pine needles. We were parked in front of a little blue house on a street filled with other little houses and lots of tall pine trees. At least a dozen cars, most of them rusted-out jalopies, were parked around the house, some even on the lawn. The shades of all the windows were drawn, but light shone around the cracks, and I heard the steady pulsing of music.

"Maybe this isn't a good idea," I said, though I didn't know where we would go as an alternative. I had never been comfortable at parties. Not that I had gone to any. My idea of a party came from movies like *Animal House*, which always seemed to playing somewhere on cable. I imagined going inside and some guy asking me where my keg was. I tried to think of a good excuse why I didn't have a keg.

"Relax," Jake said.

"Maybe we should go home," I said.

"Will you just quit?"

Gabe opened the door and we followed him into a warm living room, a distinct haze in the air. It smelled something awful, and it wasn't a smell I had ever smelled before, though I had a pretty good sense of what it was. The guys and girls lounging in the living room, passing a blue glass pipe between them, gave me a pretty good idea. There were three guys and two girls, all in their early twenties, all of them with the same glassy-eyed look about them. One of them, a black girl with dreadlocks, got up and turned off the stereo.

"Hey, man," one of them said, a pudgy guy with olive skin and slicked black hair. "How's life in the valley?"

"Satisfactory," Gabe said. They all stood there nodding until Gabe finally remembered us. "Oh, this is . . . um . . ."

76

"Jake and Charlie," Jake said.

"Riiiiight," Gabe said. "My sister's friends. They're on a sort of quest."

"Quest!" one of the other guys exclaimed, a short Hispanic guy wearing a Hawaiian shirt. "Right on! I *love* quests!"

One of the girls, a redhead, was currently using the pipe. She exhaled smoke from her nose, then closed her eyes and mumbled, "Quests are cool."

"Kind of like Gandalf," the black girl said. She wore a white T-shirt with black lettering that read, YES, BUT WHAT ABOUT ME?

"Gandalf is cool," the girl with the pipe said.

"Who's Gandalf?" the guy with the olive complexion asked.

"*Lord of the Rings*," the girl said.

"Lord of the what?"

"*The Rings*, man, *the Rings*," another guy said. He sat on a rocker in the corner, and he was dressed all in black, even wearing a black bandanna. His glasses made his eyes seem huge. "It's like totally frickin' awesome. There's like frickin' awesome special effects. There's dragons and sword fights and magic stuff—frickin' awesome. You really should see it."

"That's the movie," the girl with the pipe said.

"Huh?"

"It was a book first."

"Oh yeah. I forgot. By that British dude." He looked over at us. "Where you guys going?"

"Colorado," Jake said.

"Colorado!" the guy exclaimed. "That's frickin' awesome. You guys got a ring?"

"What?" Jake said.

"You taking the ring and throwing it in the fire, like the movie? Like Frodo and Sam?"

"No," Jake said. "Charlie's got a portrait."

"Don't," I whispered, but it was already too late.

"A what?" the guy in black said.

"A portrait," Jake said. "You know, a picture he drew. Of his dad. He wants to give it him."

"Oh," the guy in black said. He nodded thoughtfully, contemplating the floor for so long I thought the conversation was over, then looked back at me. "Why?"

I wished I could disappear. "It's just something to do," I said.

"Can we see it?" the black girl said.

"Show it to them," Jake said.

"Aw, that's okay," I said.

They all started begging and pleading for me to show it to them, and I put them off, but then Jake got down on his knees and made a fool of himself, so I had to give in. I took it out of the bag and opened it real quick, but they protested, so I opened it again and held it there while they all leaned in, squinting as if it was the size of a postage stamp. "It's not finished yet," I said.

"Wow," the black girl said.

"It's really, really good, dude," the guy with olive skin said. "Like, really, really, *really* good."

They all chimed in how good it was, and even though it was embarrassing, and I wasn't sure how well any of them could even see the picture in their current state of mind, I kind of liked it. I thanked them and put it back in the bag.

"You going to art school?" the guy in black said.

"I don't know," I said.

"My cousin's going to art school in California." He paused. "At least I think it's my cousin. It might be my roommate's cousin. Not sure."

"Charlie's going to be a lawyer," Jake said.

"A doctor," I said, sighing.

"Oh," the black girl said. "Why?"

"I hate lawyers," the guy with olive skin said.

"He said *doctor*, idiot," the black girl said. She looked at me. "So why a doctor?"

"Yeah man," the Hispanic guy said. He was now smoking the pipe. "You could be an artist or something."

"I don't know," I said. I thought about telling them that artists always ended up living in their parents' basements, then thought better of it. They seemed like just the sort of people who lived in their parents' basements.

"His dad's a doctor," Jake said.

I was beginning to get really pissed at Jake. They all stared at him for a long time, everybody nodding, though I wasn't sure exactly what they were nodding about. The silence was getting unbearable.

"So how about you guys?" I said. "What do you want to be when you grow up?"

I regretted it as soon as the words were out of my mouth. It was such a kidlike thing to say, and these "kids" were in their twenties. I braced myself for their laughter, but nobody laughed. Instead they all looked kind of thoughtful, and then after a while they looked kind of sad, as if they'd all just discovered that a bunch of friends had gone to the movies and not invited them. It was a moment I'd think about a lot, long after I left, how sad they all looked. I wasn't sure what to make of it. It made me kind of sad too, and I wasn't sure why.

"I'm working on a screenplay," the black girl said.

"I thought you finished it," the Hispanic guy said.

"Not yet," the black girl said.

"Maybe I'll be a lawyer," the guy with olive skin said, the one who had said he hated lawyers.

They fell into silence. I suddenly had the urge to bolt out of the room. Maybe I wasn't all that sure why I wanted to be a doctor, and maybe it *was* just because I wanted to be like Dad, but at least I wanted to do something. At least I had a direction. They didn't seem to have a direction at all, and it was just the kind of thing Dad (and, to a lesser degree, Mom) had warned me about: If you didn't stay focused on your future, you wouldn't have one.

On the other hand, it was like they weren't letting all the little crap that bothers most people get to them. It seemed that all Mom did was worry about little crap, and if you were never around someone who *didn't*, you got to thinking that there was no other way to be, that it was normal to spend most of your time worrying about stuff that didn't matter all that much in the grand scheme of things.

Gabe slid over next to the black girl, and she handed him the pipe. He took a good drag, then let out the smoke slowly. When he spoke, his voice sounded higher and more strained.

"You dudes want to partake in the festivities?" he said, holding up the pipe.

"Oh, that's all right," I said.

"Hell yeah," Jake said.

Gabe handed him the pipe, and Jake sat cross-legged on the carpet. I couldn't believe he'd actually do it, but Jake took a big drag, like he'd been doing it all his life. He closed his eyes and exhaled the smoke out his nose. Then he looked up at me.

"Try it, man," he said.

"That's all right."

"Come on. One hit won't kill you."

"Really, I'm fine."

"Come on, I promise it won't hurt you. Live a little. How will you know if you never try it? At least try it."

He held up the pipe. I hated that everybody was staring at me, and I hated Jake for making them stare at me. I was scared to death to do any drugs. All those public-service messages kept running through my head, and I just knew if I took one little puff of that pipe, I'd end up climbing out of the cardboard box, wearing army fatigues and no shoes, and wondering what had happened to my life. This was one of those peer pressure moments they talked about. I was supposed to just say no. But that sounded dumb, just saying no. I didn't want them to laugh at me. I just wanted them to stop staring.

"Okay," I said.

I figured I would just pretend. I'd put the pipe up to my lips and pretend to smoke it, but I wouldn't actually inhale. I realized this was what had gotten Bill Clinton in trouble years ago, but it seemed like the best choice. That made me wonder if Bill Clinton had done it for the same reason, just because he hadn't wanted to lose face in front of others.

"You really don't have to," the black girl said. "It's not for everyone."

"No, I want to," I said.

"We understand if it's a matter of principles," Gabe said. "We don't want you to violate any—"

"I want to! I really want to!"

It was strange, but the more they told me I didn't have to do it, the more I felt I *had* to do it. I knelt next to Jake, sliding off my backpack and dropping it on the floor next to him. I kept repeating to myself, don't inhale, don't inhale, and that was probably a pretty stupid thing to do, because it was like how somebody in the movies tells somebody not to look down, and of course they do, that's how it always works.

He handed me the pipe, and I put it up to my lips. The glass was warm. I tried not to think about how many other mouths had been on it. I wasn't going to inhale. I didn't *want* to inhale. But as soon as I glanced up at everyone, I couldn't stop myself. I sucked in a breath. It was just like how I got into the van with Jake, exactly the same way: I hadn't wanted to do it, but I had found myself doing it anyway.

It was like inhaling fire. I wanted to seem tough, like I could take it, but my throat was burning, and I coughed violently. My eyes filled with tears. I coughed and coughed, and when I finally stopped, I heard laughter.

"Hey, man," Jake said, "it's all right. It's always that way the first time. Try again. I don't think you even got any in your lungs."

"No, that's—" I began, and started coughing again. I handed him the pipe.

"You sure?" Jake said. "It really does get better—"

But I was already out of the room. I didn't even have time to ask where the bathroom was. Luckily, it was the first door on the left down a short hall, and I just made it to the toilet, throwing up the day's lunch into the porcelain bowl. It was only when I stopped that I saw how dirty the toilet was, a ring of yellow scum at the edge of the water, which made me throw up one more time.

I stayed in there until I got a hold of myself, dashed some water on my face, reached for the towel, and, seeing how dirty and stained the yellow towel was, used some wadded up toilet paper to dry my face instead. When I walked slowly back into the room, I expected some questions of concern, or at least sympathetic looks, only to find them exactly as I had left them, sitting in a circle, passing the pipe among them.

Jake looked up, eyes glazed. "You all right, man?"

"Yeah," I said.

"Hey," the black girl said, "it's all right. Sometimes you don't even get high the first time."

I nodded. I certainly didn't feel high. I just felt sick. A little stupid, too, since I had never wanted to smoke the pipe in the first place, only save myself a little embarrassment. Which, of course, had only led me to being more embarrassed. I wondered when I would ever learn.

The smell in the room was making me queasy again, so I tried to breathe through my mouth. Standing there, I wondered what Mom would think if she saw me. Then I realized that Mom was probably thinking of me right at that minute, and I started feeling sick again, but this time because of the guilt. "Um, does anybody have a cell phone?" I asked.

"Why?" Jake said.

"I just need to call someone."

"Who?"

"Just someone."

"You're not calling your mom, are you?"

I hated how he always seemed to guess what was going on with me. By this time, the guy with the olive skin had dug a silver phone out of his pocket, and he handed it to me. "Just don't call any 1-900 numbers," he said, chuckling.

"Dude," Jake said, "don't call your mom."

"I'm not calling my mom," I said.

"Then who are you calling?"

"I'm . . . all right, I'm calling my mom. But I just want her to know I'm okay."

"That's so sweet," the redheaded girl said, then took another puff from the pipe. "Maybe we should all call our moms. And wish them Happy Mother's Day."

"That's two months away," the black girl said.

"Still," the redheaded girl said, "it'd be awfully nice."

"Charlie—" Jake began.

"I'll just be a second," I said, and retreated around the corner, into the kitchen. I took my backpack with me. I'm sure that looked strange, me taking my backpack with me to the kitchen, but I wasn't all that comfortable leaving it in the room with a bunch of potheads.

The yellow linoleum floor was coming up at the edges, peeling away from the walls. Dirty dishes and pizza boxes were piled on the countertops and the sink. It wasn't very private, so I crossed the room and opened the sliding glass door, stepping onto a wooden deck and closing the door behind me. A weak porch light lit up a small area of the gray-weathered boards. A high chain-link fence surrounded a yard that was cloaked in darkness.

The night was cool, a breeze swaying the tops of the pine trees. I flipped open the phone, took a few deep breaths, then dialed our home number. I was hoping she wasn't home, so I could just leave a message. She answered on the first ring.

"Hello?" she said.

She sounded worried. I swallowed hard.

"Mom?" I said.

"Oh God, oh God, Charlie, oh God, I've been worried sick—where are you?" It all came out in one breathless rush, and she was already crying. There might have been more *oh Gods* in there. It was hard to keep track.

"I'm okay, Mom," I said.

"Oh God, are you hurt? What happened? Oh God, I've been worried to death. Do you need me to come pick you up?"

"No, I'm okay, Mom. I'm fine. I just . . . wanted to tell you I was okay."

"Did—Did that Tucker boy beat you up? Did he force you to get into the car with him? I knew you'd never do that on your own. Where—Where are you? I'll come get you right away. You just tell me." She was crying so much it was hard to understand her.

"Jake didn't force me," I said. "He helped me. A guy named Leo—"

"It doesn't matter, it doesn't matter. All that matters is that you're safe. Where are you? Oh God, we'll get you out of this mess. Mr. Harkin has promised not to press charges if you agree to certain things. It'll be fine. It won't affect your school record. He promised me." I heard her blow her nose into a handkerchief. "Now where are you? Who's this Bernie Melman?"

"Who?" I said.

"The name on the caller I.D. Who is he?"

I felt a sickening feeling in the pit of my stomach. I hadn't thought about caller I.D. Now she had a name. With a little bit of work, she'd find out where that name lived, and then she'd pressure good old Bernie to tell her where I went.

It meant our whole trip was doomed from the start.

It meant there was no reason not to have her come get me right away.

But, strange as it was, I still wasn't ready to go home. I had every reason to go home, but I wanted to press on more than ever. It may have started as a lark, but somewhere along the line something had changed inside me. Was *still* changing. I couldn't say what exactly, but something was definitely changing, and I didn't want it to stop. I didn't know if I was really going to make it all the way to Denver, but I didn't want to go back to my old life. Not yet. Not now.

"Charlie?" Mom said. "What's going on?"

"I'm just going on a little trip, Mom."

"A trip? A trip where?"

"Just someplace. I have to do something."

"What? What do you have to do?"

"I really don't want to say. I just . . . I want you to know I'm fine. I'm okay. I don't want you to worry. I'll call again when I can."

86

"Charlie," she said more sternly, "this isn't some kind of joke, is it? Because if it is—"

"It's not a joke," I said.

She was silent a long time. "Will you please tell me what's going on?"

I was thinking about what to tell her when I heard a rustling out in the darkness of the yard and then a jingling. I froze. It hadn't dawned on me the chain-link fence was there for a reason until a big black mastiff came loping out of the shadows, the metal tags hanging from its collar clinking. The dog—it was hard to call it a dog when it was as big as a small horse—walked up on the deck, gazing at me with its big black eyes. We were practically at eye level. A line of slobber hung from the corner of its mouth like a gooey rubber band. Its tail wasn't wagging, which wasn't a good sign. It took me a second to realize the dog had only three legs.

"Oh no," I said.

"Charlie?" Mom said, obviously detecting the worry in my voice. "Charlie, what is it?"

"Uh, nothing, I just . . ."

The mastiff took a few steps toward me.

"G-Good boy," I said. "Nice dog."

"What dog?" Mom said. "Charlie, answer me!"

The mastiff jumped up and I screamed. It was a real whopper of a scream, long and high-pitched, like a woman in one of those slasher flicks. But the dog didn't attack. It began to whine and lick my face, front paws on my shoulders as if we were going to dance, tail now wagging furiously. In the onslaught of affection,

I dropped the phone, and it clacked against the deck. I heard my mother screaming hysterically.

"Charlie!" she cried. "Charlie! Oh God, what's happening? Oh God, oh God . . ."

I was drowning in a shower of drool, and the dog's breath was awful, like the inside of an outhouse. If you wanted to get a prisoner to talk, there was no need for any other form of torture. After only a few seconds, I would have given up all of our national secrets just for the promise of a hot bath. By the time I managed to get the dog down, I heard the screen door behind me open. I turned, and there was Jake, looking dazed. His long hair had fallen in front of his eyes.

"What happened?" he said.

"Charlie! Charlie!" came Mom's tiny voice below.

I reached for the phone, but the mastiff took it as a sign that I wanted to play, and he put his head between me and the phone. More slobbering ensued. Meanwhile, Jake snatched up the phone.

"No!" I said. "Give me—"

"Mrs. Hill?" he said. "This is Jake. Charlie's fine. Only smoked pot once, and I don't think he really inhaled much. Talk to you later."

I pushed the dog away and lunged for the phone, but it was too late; he'd already clicked off. I ripped the phone away and glared at him, but it was no good; it was like glaring at someone who'd just woken from a long nap. Still, I was so pissed that I was really going to let him have it, maybe even throw in a few swear words, but before I could, I heard a deep male voice yell from the living room.

"*Stay where you are! You're under arrest!*"

That woke Jake up. He jerked upright like a wind-up soldier and then looked at me, mouthing the word *cops*. So this was it, I thought. Regardless of what I'd told Mom, it was all going to end before we'd even gotten started.

But Jake wasn't thinking about giving up. He bolted down the steps and headed for the fence.

"Where're you going?" I said.

"Run!" he said.

"We can't—"

"Run!"

Beyond the reach of the light, he was nothing but a dark shape. I watched that shape leap up and over the fence like a gymnast who'd been doing it all his life. Heart pounding, I followed because I didn't know what else to do. I had a little more trouble climbing the chain-link, and when I reached the top, the mastiff bit down on my backpack, tugging at me. *Grr, grr, grr.* It was a friendly growl, like it thought it was a game. I knew the mastiff would bring the cops outside soon, and, panicking, I swatted at the dog. This must have surprised him as much as it did me, because he let me go. With a great effort, I scaled the fence and stumbled over, falling, skinning my palms on a concrete sidewalk. Then I sprang up, running again.

Down a strange dark street.

Following Jake.

For the second time that day, running from the cops and following Jake.

If that wasn't a sign I was supposed to stop hanging around him, I didn't know what was.

chapter nine

Jake angled across one of the lawns onto a side street and disappeared around the corner. Dogs yipped at us from the safety of their fenced-in yards. A man and a woman were yelling at each other in their kitchen. I followed after Jake, huffing and puffing my way there, and nearly ran past him. The street lamp above us was out, and Jake was hiding behind a boxy motor home parked on the street. I could just barely make out the fringes of his blond hair and his jean jacket.

I ducked in next to him, leaning against the cool metal, gasping for breath. He put a finger to his lips and cocked his head, listening. I didn't hear anything except the barking dogs and the buzzing of a nearby electric box. The sweat on my face turned cold in the night breeze.

"I don't think they're following us," he whispered.

"You know," I said, breathing hard, "this running from the police thing is starting to get old."

"Really? And here I thought we were just starting to get good at it."

"What're we going to do? We don't have anywhere to stay."

"We'll wait here. Just for a few minutes. Make sure the cops aren't coming."

"Where are we going to stay? I thought we were going to crash there for the night. We don't have any—"

"I don't know, Charlie, okay!"

I let it drop for the time being, figuring he'd let me in on some sort of plan when the time was right. My backpack felt as if it was filled with bricks. It was all the tomelike textbooks in there, and I thought about how silly it was, running from cops with a bunch of textbooks. When it was obvious the cops weren't coming, Jake started walking. The moon was up high by now, and I had butterflies in my stomach, because I didn't even know what time it was. It must have been late. Eventually, I couldn't push the doubts away any longer, and I asked Jake again what we were going to do.

He sighed. "I don't know. How about get a hotel room?"

"A hotel room?" I said.

"Yeah. I've got money. We'll stay the night, then maybe take a bus in the morning. Too late to do anything else tonight, don't you think?"

"Um yeah. I guess you're right."

"Don't worry. We'll get two beds."

"I wasn't worried," I said.

"Yeah, you were. I could tell. You were wondering if I was some kind of homo. Look, here's a main road. There's got to be one down here."

It wasn't much of a main road, just two lanes with a couple of gas stations, a mini mart, a Denny's, and there, a couple blocks down, a Motel 6. I tried to imagine walking inside the motel, arranging for a room, and then actually staying the night—without Mom or Rick or Dad or anybody else to chaperone. Just the two of us. I couldn't see it. But then there we were, walking along the deserted street, our skin looking chalky in the moonlight, only the occasional car rumbling past. In moments we were at the hotel. It was two stories, maybe two dozen rooms, all with orange outside doors. Only about a third of the parking spots were full. The pool was covered and dark.

Jake stopped at the sidewalk path to the motel office and looked at me. He didn't say anything, but there was still a question on his face: *You ready?* I looked at the motel, feeling my heart pound a little harder, wondering just what the hell I was doing in Bend, Oregon, about to stay in a motel with a guy who'd once broken my Game Boy and still hadn't apologized for it. Stranger things may have happened, but I couldn't think of any at the moment.

"You sure you have enough money?" I asked.

"I've got more than enough," he said.

"But you don't have to spend it. I'm sure you've got other stuff—"

"I want to."

"Yeah, but on a motel room?" I said. "You could always buy stuff you want. It's a lot of money."

Jake didn't say anything for a minute. An old gray truck passed, kicking up dust and dirt. "What is it, Charlie?" he said.

"Huh?"

"I'm getting the feeling maybe you don't want to do this."

I heard the rattle of wheels across the street. I looked and saw a homeless man pushing a shopping cart, emerging from the shadows behind the mini-mart. It was just coincidence, I guess, but it did get me thinking. Could that be me a little ways down the road? He was hairy enough that somebody might mistake him for Bigfoot, except Bigfoot didn't wear clothes and this guy had on enough clothes to make it through an Alaskan winter. Of course, that might be how Bigfoot had eluded capture all these years. Maybe he had just put on some clothes and had started pushing a shopping cart.

After the excitement of almost getting caught by the police for the second time, I *was* having second thoughts. My thinking was that I had pushed it as far as I could. I wanted to be some kind of James Dean rebel, wanted to be bold and deliver the drawing to Dad in person, travel across the country, have adventures, but I was realizing it just wasn't me. It was like I'd fallen into a raging river, and I'd just let it carry me along for a while, but now I was on the shore. If I continued from here, it was by my own choice, and not because I was letting it happen.

"I don't want to be a party pooper," I said.

He snorted. "Party pooper? What are you, in fifth grade? Nobody talks like that. You want to go back? Just spit it out, if that's what you want." He pulled a cigarette out of his jacket pocket and lit it up with a little yellow lighter. He took a few puffs, blowing it out of the side of his mouth. "Come on, man, just say it."

"Yeah," I said.

"Yeah what?"

"Yeah, I want to go back."

He shook his head. "Unbelievable. Come on, live a little!"

"I just . . . I've got to go home, Jake. This is just too crazy for me."

"Uh-huh. Let me ask you something. Are you happy right now?"

I shrugged. "Sure, I guess."

"Sure, you guess?"

"Yeah."

"You *guess* you're happy."

"Right."

"Like, you're not sure."

I snorted. "What are you, a fucking shrink?"

My use of the *f*-word shocked both of us. I couldn't remember if I'd ever said it out loud before. Even weirder, it felt good saying it.

"Ah, profanity," he said with a small smile. "Slowly, we make progress."

"Oh, fuck off."

"Don't overdo it, now," he said. "A little too much, and you might end up like me. A *real* loser." He took another few drags of his cigarette, smiling a little, looking at me the way you might look at a science project that had come out the way you'd hoped. "Look, man," he went on, "I'm not going to try to convince you anymore. I'm just saying you should trust your instincts. If you're happy, go with it. Stop worrying so much. But if you still want to go home, then go. Call your mom or whatever. I'm sure she'll come get you."

He didn't sound condescending, like he was trying to make me feel bad for running home to mama. He sounded fed up.

"She can take you home too," I said.

"Oh no," he said. "I can't go home."

"Huh? What do you mean, *can't?*"

"I can't go back," he said. "At least not right now. Not for a while."

"Why?"

He kicked at the curb. "Well, see, it's about the money. There's something I didn't tell you."

"Yeah?"

"I might have . . . well, I might have stole it."

"Stole it!" I said, even though I'd kind of thought he might have taken it from someone. "Well, you'll just give it back."

"It's not that easy," he said. "See, my foster mom, she's kind of a slut—"

"Jake!"

"Well, sorry, but it's true. When my foster dad's out driving his truck, she's always sleeping with somebody. Like, every night almost. And I kind of stole it from one of her boyfriends. Right out of his pants, before I left for school today."

"I don't understand why—"

"And he's a drug dealer. Kind of big one, really. And he has guns. Lots of them."

I fell silent, digesting what he'd said. "Well, it wasn't a lot of money, just a couple hundred—"

"Yeah, I kind of lied about that, too. I've got over five thousand."

It was like I'd just found myself in some kind of gangster movie, but I didn't know my lines. This sort of thing didn't happen to somebody sixteen years old, at least not somebody like me, somebody who would probably break into a cold sweat if he even stole a paper clip. Five thousand dollars. From a drug dealer. Drug dealers killed people for that sort of thing. If I'd been in a daze since leaving Rexton, this was like the smelling salts that brought me back to reality.

"Oh God," I said. "Oh God, oh God." Now I sounded like my mother, which made me feel even worse.

"Hey, man," he said, "you don't look so good."

"I think I'm going to throw up. I can't believe you did that! Is it really that much?"

He pulled the wad of bills out of his front pocket. When he flipped through them, I saw that there were a few twenties on top, but mostly it was hundreds. The world felt like it was tilting. I sat down on the curb. The concrete felt cold through my jeans, and then I felt cold all over. The homeless man was a couple of blocks away now, but I could still hear the rattle of his cart. Now I didn't see him as a possible future. I actually wanted to *be* him. At least he probably didn't have to worry about getting iced by some drug dealer.

"You've got to give it back," I said.

"Man, I can't," he said. "If I give back the money, how am I supposed to get around?"

"You don't! You go home!"

He shook his head. "You're not getting it. If I go home, he'll kill me. Put me in a ditch somewhere."

"Not if you give back the money!"

Jake sat down on the curb next to me, crossing his legs so that his knees touched the road. He took a long drag on his cigarette, then let it out slowly. The pockmarks on his cheeks, filled with shadows, gave him leopardlike skin. "Look," he said, "I'm not giving it back. It's my starting-over money."

"Your what?"

"My starting-over money," he said. A rusted-out VW bug rumbled past, the loud engine making it impossible to talk. When it was gone, Jake took a few more puffs on the cigarette. He was trying to look cool, but there was something in his eyes that made him seem just like a scared little kid. "I can't go back to that life," he said quietly. "I can't. I'm going to do something great, and I need some money to do it."

"What are you going to do?"

"I've got some ideas."

"Well, like what?"

"Just some stuff. You know, some things I've been playing around with." He looked at me. "I didn't tell you this before, but there's somebody I want to see too. He lives in Cheyenne, and it's really not that far from Denver. I thought we could go see him after, you know, we see your dad. He said he'd help me get going, you know, get my feet off the ground. He's also my uncle."

"Your uncle?" I asked.

"Yeah." He stubbed out his cigarette. "My dad's brother. They didn't get along. Bruce—that's my dad's brother—he's really successful. He owns all kinds of businesses. He told me if I ever showed up on his doorstep when I was all grown, he'd help me get set up. Told me at the big family reunion deal we did one summer way back. It was like the only time I saw him."

I wanted to say, *because your dad ran off?* But I remembered how he had reacted when I'd mentioned his father before. "He'd get you set up doing what?"

Jake shrugged. "Who cares? It'll be better than hanging around Rexton, that's for sure." He sighed. "Here's what I'll do. If you come with me, I promise I'll send the money back after we see Uncle Bruce. I bet I can even get Uncle Bruce to spot me whatever I spent so far, so my foster mom's boyfriend will get the whole five thousand. If he gets everything back, you won't have anything to worry about."

"You think he'd do that? Give you the money?"

"Probably. Sure." He must have seen the look on my face, because he went on. "Look, I don't know him that well. Just met him like that one time, really. But he was very nice. I got the feeling he cared about what happened to me. Like he knew my parents were shit heads."

"Jake!"

"Well, it's true. They're big-time shit heads and everybody knows it."

"Yeah, well, you still shouldn't say it."

"Why not?" he said, and I could see the challenge on his face. "I see my mom maybe a couple times a year, and she's so baked she usually doesn't remember me. And Dad . . ." I thought I was finally going to learn what was going on with his dad, but he just shook his head. "And my foster parents, they're dickwads too. I can't go back, Charlie. I'm going to see Uncle Bruce. I was just waiting for my chance. It was just luck that I ended up with the money on the same day you were going to get pounded by Leo. And then when I saw that portrait, I thought, *Hey, why not both of us go.* Two birds with one stone, you know." He laughed. "The Water Balloon Boys on one last great getaway."

There were holes in his story. I couldn't say exactly what they were, but there were definitely holes. And yet, he *did* have that money, and it was a lot of money. That made me think at least that part of the story was true, him stealing from the drug dealer. Which meant that drug dealer probably knew by now that I took off with Jake in Mr. Harkin's Mustang. If I went back, he was definitely going to come looking for me. He would want to know where the money was, and he wouldn't be nice about it. Those types of people don't just go away when you politely tell them you don't know.

So what choice did I have? I had to go with Jake, at least until he sent the money back. And if we were going in that direction, then I might as well see Dad and give him the portrait. Maybe Jake would end up getting his life going in a new direction too. He may have broken my Game Boy, but he had ended up with a much more rotten life than me, and that was saying something.

"One last getaway," I said. "All right, I'll go. But you have to promise to mail the money back, no matter what. Even if your uncle slams the door in your face, you have to send it back."

He sighed. "All right, fine."

"You promise?"

"I promise, I promise!" He raised his hand, his face solemn. "Scout's honor, I'll send it back, no matter what."

"Were you ever in the Scouts?"

He looked sheepish. "Well . . ."

"I didn't think so."

"Hey, I can still promise like a Boy Scout, can't I?"

It was the kind of dumb thing you had to laugh at, even if you were standing on a deserted road in the middle of the night, a long way from home.

chapter ten

Twenty minutes later, we were stretching out on our own double beds in a room that smelled like it had once been underwater, each of us wolfing down a cheeseburger and fries we had bought from the Burger King next door. There was a moment of panic when the hotel clerk had asked for some identification, but then Jake whipped out some fake I.D. and the guy didn't bat an eyelash, just took Jake's deposit money and gave him the keys. I was amazed Jake had fake I.D., but I knew I should have expected it.

I hadn't realized how hungry I was until we went to our room and I caught a whiff of the grilling burgers on the night's breeze. Jake must have realized the same thing, because he headed for the restaurant without me even asking.

The carpet in the hotel room was the color of rust, and it was so thin it looked like paint. The chairs and table must have been around since the fifties, and they'd been heavily used in all that time. The steady drip from the faucet in the bathroom would most likely drive me insane during the night. But all in all, it was better than sleeping under a bridge. Even the wet, moldy smell wasn't so bad once we were eating. On the little television, we watched an old Clint Eastwood Western, which was the only decent thing on.

The digital clock between the two beds read 11:38. It was hard to believe that everything that had happened so far had happened in under ten hours. It seemed like a lifetime's worth of stuff. Maybe ten lifetimes' worth of stuff.

"So," Jake said through a mouthful of cheeseburger, "you know what you're going to say to your dad when you see him?"

"Not really," I said, using a napkin to wipe some stray ketchup off my chin.

"You gonna ask him if you can live with him?"

"Huh?"

He shoved some fries into his mouth. When he spoke, it was mostly garbled. "Lib wid 'im," he said.

"Why would I want to live with him?"

He swallowed. The lump was big enough that I could actually see his throat move. "I don't know," he said. "I thought maybe that was why you wanted to give him the portrait."

"I don't want to live with him," I said.

"Okay."

"I just wanted to give him the picture."

"All right."

We lapsed into silence. It was true that I was going to have to say something to Dad. I really had no idea what that was going to be. Except for the phone calls on my birthday and on Christmas, when we mostly followed the same script (*"How are you, son?"* *"Fine, Dad."* *"Good, good, glad to hear it, how are your grades?"* *"Good, Dad."*), we hadn't had a real conversation since my cat Streak had gotten hit by a car when I was ten. And *that* had been only because Mom had forced him to talk to me about life and death and what it all means, which were the exact words I had overheard her say to him when he had come home from work. *"Dear, you need to talk to your son about life and death and what it all means."*

I don't remember what he had said, but I do remember the conversation had lasted about thirty seconds. He'd said he had a few important phone calls to make (how important could they be, when you're a dentist?), but I had later found him with a beer in hand in front of the television in the basement, watching the Oakland A's take on the Texas Rangers.

It was making me nervous, trying to think of what to say to him. I just wanted to see what he did when I handed him the picture. As far as I knew, he didn't even know I could draw.

We finished our dinner, and it wasn't long before my eyelids started to feel heavy. It turned out I didn't have to worry much about brushing my teeth or sleeping without pajamas, because when I woke again, the room was dark and Jake was snoring. My neck was sore, and my stomach felt like there were rocks in it. I shuffled to the bathroom and took care of business, still barely half-awake. My head felt stuffy.

When I came out of the bathroom, before I flicked off the bathroom light, I saw that Jake was under the covers, his jacket and jeans on the floor next to the bed. Which meant he was down to his underwear. I wasn't all that comfortable taking off my clothes around anyone, even somebody who was sleeping, so I got under the covers first, then took off my pants, folded them, and carefully placed them on the floor where I could get to them quickly.

I lay there for a while, the bedspread tucked up to my chin, and stared at the ceiling in the dark. The room now smelled like greasy fries. The light from the parking lot rimmed the curtains. After a while my eyes adjusted, allowing me to see everything in the room.

I thought about Mom. I wondered if she was asleep, or if she was just sitting by the phone, waiting for me to call. That killed me, thinking about her, so I started counting goats jumping over a log. I'm not much of a sheep guy, so it's always goats for me. Since Dad had left, I'd had a lot of trouble sleeping, so I'd probably counted a million goats.

I was up to two hundred goats when I heard someone crying. It was soft and muffled. At first I thought it might be Jake. But the longer I listened, the more I realized it was coming from right behind me, through the wall. It would stop for a while, then start again. I tried to ignore it, but it's pretty much impossible to sleep when there's someone crying near you.

"Z'at you?" Jake said. His voice was slurred.

"No," I said. "It's somebody in the next room."

He was silent a moment. "Sounds like a girl. I wonder what she's upset about."

"I don't know."

I heard him roll over in his bed. The person crying stopped long enough that I thought maybe she was done, then she started again.

"Think we should go see what's wrong?" Jake asked.

"No," I said.

"She might want someone to talk to."

"I just—I just don't think we should bother her."

She went on crying. It was a really pitiful sound. I remembered Mom making that sound a long time ago, right after Dad had left. I remembered hearing it late at night, all the way down the hall. Even when I'd covered my ears, I still couldn't block it.

I heard a rustle of blankets, then pants being zipped. I saw Jake's shadowy outline on the edge of the bed.

"What're you doing?" I said.

"Going over there," Jake said.

He slipped on shoes and put on his jacket. I turned on the bedside lamp, squinting as my eyes adjusted. Jake was already at the door.

"I really don't think you should do this," I said.

"I'll be back in a second."

"Jake—"

He was already out the door. I sat there, feeling pissed, not knowing if I should try to fall sleep or just wait until he came back. Through the wall, I heard Jake's knock, and the crying stopped. I sat up on my knees and put my ear against the wall, cupping it with my hands. The wall felt cool against my ear. The knock came again. I heard a girl's voice, but I couldn't understand her. I heard Jake saying something, but I couldn't understand him, either. Then I heard what sounded like her door unlocking. She talked. He talked. Then there was silence.

It made me crazy wondering what was going on over there. Then I heard a click behind me, and I turned just as Jake and a short dark-skinned girl entered the room.

"Uh . . . ," Jake said.

I realized I was kneeling there in my tighty-whities. I dropped like a rock, jerking the covers up to my waist. "Hi," I said in a small voice.

"This is Charlie," Jake said. "Charlie, this is Anju. I told her she could hang with us for a while."

104

Anju gave me a weak smile. She had a foreign look, maybe Indian or Pakistani or Filipino. The skin under her eyes was streaked with mascara. She was so tiny, and so thin, that standing there, wringing her hands, she made me think of a lost little four-year-old. She could have been sixteen or twenty-six; it was hard to tell. Her hair had the unnatural red tint of someone who dyed it, and it was tied back in a ponytail except for a loose strand that curled down to her lips. They were small, pouty lips, with red lipstick a few shades too bright. She wore a rumpled red sweatshirt, unzipped, and underneath a red T-shirt with some kind of dragon design. Her green capri pants came down to the middle of her calves, and her red sandals made me think of the kind that Dorothy wore in The Wizard of Oz. I saw that her toenails were painted the same bright shade of red.

"Nice to meet you," I said.

"I'm—I'm sorry about the noise." She had a very slight accent.

Jake made a *pfff* sound. "Don't worry about it. Why don't you take a load off for a while. Charlie there was getting lonely."

"I really don't want to bother you," she said. One of her front teeth slightly overlapped the other one.

"I told you," Jake said, "you're not bothering us. Isn't that right, Charlie? We were just up anyway."

"Right," I said.

Jake motioned to one of the orange bucket chairs facing the beds. "Go for it," he said. "Please. I'd be crushed if you didn't." He placed his hand over his heart.

She let out a little giggle. "Okay," she said. "Just for a few minutes."

"You want any water or anything?"

"No."

"Beer?"

She giggled again, settling into the chair. When she smiled, she did it with her lips closed, and when she laughed, she covered her mouth with her hands. "How old are you anyway?"

"Me? I'm only eleven. But Charlie there's pushing forty."

"Well, you both look like you should be in high school."

Jake lunged onto the bed. He propped up a pillow, then turned around to face her. "Just graduated, actually. We're doing a little trip to celebrate. So what brings you to Bend?"

"Oh," she said, shrugging.

She stared at the floor, tapping one of her feet. The look on her face, it was like she'd just heard her best friend died. There was an uncomfortable silence and I tried to think of something to say. Nothing came to me. I was still a little irritated that Jake had invited her over at all. Why did we have to get involved in her life? We didn't know her.

"I bet it's to join the circus," Jake said.

She looked up, confused. "What?"

"Trapeze artist, right?" he said, smiling.

"No," she said, laughing.

"Lion tamer? You definitely look like a lion tamer."

She shook her head. When she was laughing or smiling, her whole face changed. She still wasn't exactly beautiful, but she was pretty. It made me think of Kari, too, how she seemed pretty when she smiled.

"It's much more lame," she said. "I was just in town seeing somebody. A . . . guy."

"Oh," Jake said knowingly, "I get it. A boyfriend."

"Yeah," Anju said. "Well, kind of. He was. Not anymore. I thought . . . well, not anymore." She had that sad look again.

"You want to talk about it?" Jake said.

She shrugged.

"You dump him or he dump you?" Jake asked.

"It was kind of mutual," she said, and she continued looking at the floor while she spoke. "Well, I guess it was more him. Him dumping me. Yeah, it was mostly that." She didn't say anything for a long time, so long that I wondered if we were just going to sit like that for the rest of the night, the three of us listening to the faucet drip in the other room, until finally she spoke again, much more softly than before. "We broke up a couple months ago . . . back in Boise. We were going to get married this summer, and then he comes out and says he needs a little space. A little breathing room. That's what he said. . . . And then he up and moves to Bend with another guy who got a job working at Mount Bachelor. He said it was just for a little while, just until he sorted some things out. Do a little snowboarding and clear his head . . . I thought I'd come out here and surprise him." Her eyes had a watery film to them.

"And?" Jake said. I couldn't believe how blunt he was. The girl was pouring her guts out, and he was acting like he wanted the next installment from Netflix.

She shrugged. "Her name is Ruth. She's the one who answered the door."

"Oh," Jake said. "Well, that sucks."

"Yeah," Anju said.

"Screw him," Jake said.

"Huh?"

"Forget the bastard. He's not worth it. I mean, how could he go out with a girl named Ruth, anyway? As far as names go, it's totally lame. Right up there with Priscilla and Gertrude in lameness. She must have been a total cow."

"Well . . ."

"Even if she *wasn't*," Jake went on quickly, "she's certainly going to be a cow before long. Because anyone with a name like Ruth is going to be a cow. It's pretty much a guarantee. You really should feel sorry for the guy. It's all downhill from here for the rest of his life. You were the best he ever could have had, and he blew it."

I didn't think there was any way to pull her back from that sad and lonely place you could see in her eyes with a lot of phony pep talk. But when she looked up, there was just a flicker of a smile on her face, not an outright smile, just a hint, and that's when I realized that even when people know the pep talk is phony, they still want to hear it. Maybe it was easier to believe a lie when somebody else was saying it rather than you saying it to yourself.

"She *did* kind of have a big nose," she said.

"There you go!" Jake said. "I bet it was a total honker. Like she'd knock people over if she turned around too fast."

"She had a body to die for though," Anju said.

"Hey now!" Jake said. "Remember, she's going to be one fat mama before long. She's going to be so fat, they'll have to lift her out of the house with one of those cranes they use to build skyscrapers. They'll have to buy a semi-truck just so they can haul her around in the trailer. And their kids! Their kids will be big roly-polies with big ugly noses!"

She had been starting to brighten up, but at the mention of kids, all the cheer went right out of her. Her eyes got watery again, and her whole body sagged.

"Not that they'll have kids!" Jake said quickly, obviously realizing his mistake. "I mean, I doubt they'll even be able to have sex, she'll be so fat." Mentioning sex made her slump even more. It was like he was delivering body blows. He went on talking even faster. "And hey, no matter how bad things are, they're not that bad. Take—take Charlie here. He's still a virgin. How lame is that?"

I could have died right on the spot. I didn't even want to look at Anju, because I was afraid that she was going to be looking at me as if I was the most pathetic person in the world.

"Wow," she said, "that's actually pretty cool."

There was no scorn in her voice. I braved a glance at her, and she didn't have a look of pity on her face. She really did look genuinely impressed.

"Um, thanks," I said.

"Too many people rush into it," she said. "It's not bad to just wait until it's the right time. I kinda wished I would have waited a little."

"Yeah," I said, as if that had been my thinking on it all along. The only problem was, I wasn't a virgin *by choice*. It had just kind of worked out that way by default. Still, I didn't want to burst her bubble.

"Hey, I got an idea," Jake said. I was afraid he was going to say something else to embarrass me, but it turned out he had something else on his mind. "Charlie and I, we need to get to Denver, and Boise's pretty much on the way, right?"

Anju nodded. "Pretty much."

"Well," Jake said, "it seems like you need some cheering up, and you know, we're happy to help. I think we're doing a pretty good job, if you don't mind my saying so."

"Oh you do, huh?" she said.

"Yeah. Just think how much better you'll feel after spending more time with us. So here's what I'm thinking: We hitch a ride with you to Boise, and you get the full benefit of our cheering up for a whole lot longer. What do you think about that? We'll even pay for gas, how about that? What a deal."

You could see her turning it over in her mind. I was amazed with how Jake had turned what really was just begging for a ride into something that made us seem generous. It was complete fakery, of course, and I'm sure she could see that, but I was still impressed with how he had done it. I probably would have just come right out and said, "Please, please, give us a ride," but his way was a lot more creative.

Finally, she shrugged. "Okay."

"Cool," Jake said.

"So you don't have a car?"

"Us?" Jake said. "Nah. We don't believe in cars. They're hard on the environment, you know."

That was the problem with Jake. He never knew when to quit.

Anju hung out in our room another hour, just shooting the breeze about important stuff like why Coke was better than Pepsi and whether Vin Diesel could really act, and by then I was so wired that I couldn't settle my mind down. I lay there in the dark, listening to the occasional truck rumble by on the road, a few hotel doors opening and closing, some footsteps passing by on the sidewalk outside, but mostly silence. Jake didn't have any problems, though. Ten minutes after turning out the light, I heard his breathing become deep and regular. When you're sleeping in the same room as someone who's sleeping, and you can't sleep, it makes you angry that that they're able to sleep when you're not. Which, of course, only makes it harder to fall asleep.

Jake finally rolled out of bed a little after nine in morning—I had been watching a *Little House on the Prairie* marathon with the volume muted, while working on Dad's portrait—and we got cleaned up and headed next door. My head felt like it was stuffed with cotton balls, and the back of my eyelids felt as sticky as fly-paper. Anju was just finished packing her little tan suitcase. Steam hung in the air from her shower, and her hair, loose instead of in a ponytail, still looked slick. She wore a white sleeveless T-shirt and blue jeans rolled up at the hems. The dark circles under her eyes made me wonder if she'd slept either.

About ten o'clock, we'd managed to check out of the hotel

and pile into her silver Honda Accord, me in the back, and head east on Highway 20. The sky was a dirty gray with strange circular cloud streaks that made me think of a manhole cover. The inside of the car smelled strongly of cigarettes.

"I don't smoke," she said, as if she was expecting us to ask. "I just bought this from a guy who smoked, that's why it smells."

"Smoking should be banned everywhere," Jake said. "Nasty habit."

I wondered if Jake even had to put out any effort to lie, or whether it was something that happened automatically for him, like sneezing. I was tired of letting him get away with it all the time.

"That's funny," I said. "I kind of remember you having some cigarettes just yesterday."

Anju laughed. I expected Jake to get angry, but he just shrugged.

"I was just smoking so you'd feel comfortable," he said.

"I don't smoke, Jake."

"Oh sure, I know. Still."

I wasn't quite ready to let it go. "Still what?"

"Oh. You know. You have this certain image of me. I just didn't want to, you know, change your image of me. When so much other stuff was happening. Thought it would be easier. Enough change as it was. Give you something to count on. The old Jake, still the same."

I wanted to keep nailing him to the wall, but then we might have to explain to Anju the real purpose of our trip, plus maybe the whole Leo incident, and I didn't want to do that. Instead, I simmered in silence.

We soon cleared town and were out in the desert country east of Bend. The land on either side of the highway was flat and desolate, wide stretches of sagebrush interrupted by a few juniper trees now and then, a band of purple hills way off in the distance. We saw some herds of cattle. The farther we went, the fewer cars we saw, until it was just the occasional mud-caked SUV with wide-eyed tourists behind the wheel or old dented trucks driven by burly guys with faces like worn leather.

Jake and Anju kept talking, but it was hard to hear from the back with all the road noise, so I just gave up and let myself daydream. I found myself thinking about Dad again, wondering how he was going to react when I gave him the picture. Every time I tried to imagine how it was going to be, my heart started to pound and my hands felt sweaty. I don't know why. Sometimes, in my fantasies, he would cry and sweep me up in a big bear hug, then tell me how sorry he was he hadn't been there for me, how it was just a big misunderstanding and we'd work it all out. In almost all of my fantasies, he asked me to come live with him. I always told him I had to think about it.

Anju was a fast driver, and we made good time, cresting a small hill and pulling into the little town of Burns, Oregon, around noon. The place made Bend seem like New York City. There were a few more trees and bushes than out in the desert country, but it was still pretty sparse compared to all the lush green back in Rexton. Everybody was hungry. We cruised past a grocery store, a hardware store, and a couple of banks, skipped a couple of ma-and-pa-type diners, finally settling on the Dairy Queen—because, like Jake said, at least you knew what you were going to get.

Ahead of us in line, there were a half-dozen guys in cowboy hats. Anju took the opportunity to duck into the restroom. Standing there in line, Jake leaned over and whispered to me.

"Dude, we really have to watch her," he said.

"Huh?"

"She's messed up, man. Really down. I'm worried about her."

"Well sure," I said. "Her boyfriend dumped her. Of course she's going to be down."

He shook his head. "It's really bad, though. You can tell. She just . . . she kind of drifts off sometimes when she's talking, and you can just see how sad she is. I'm telling you, she might do something stupid."

"Like what?"

He gave me a look like I was the densest person in the world. "Think about it, Chuckster."

"You mean like . . . commit suicide?"

"Shh. Yeah, something like that. I just get this feeling, that's all. She was down before, but something's changed. We just need to watch her."

I was a little jealous that he already felt he knew Anju well enough to be able to detect a subtle change in her mood, and I planned to insist that I ride up front the rest of the way to Boise.

Anju came back and we ordered, me and Jake getting burgers, Anju some fries and a side salad. Then Jake took off to the restroom, leaving me and Anju alone in one of the orange plastic booths. I thought, Now, here's my chance, I can try to connect with her without Jake around. But I couldn't think of anything to say. She smiled at me, then picked up the blue triangular thing with our number on it and clicked her fingernails on the hard plastic.

"So," she said.

"Yeah," I said. Already the conversation was really rolling.

"Going on a road trip, huh?"

"Yeah."

She nodded as if this was a really deep answer. "Jake said you were going to Denver."

"That's right."

"Why are you going there?"

"I don't know," I said.

"Oh."

That pretty much killed the conversation. The problem was, I wasn't very good at lying, so instead of just making up an answer like Jake would, to keep things rolling, I had to answer with, "I don't know." I could tell her the truth, of course, but I wasn't willing to do that yet. And there wasn't much she could do with "I don't know," which left us both twiddling our thumbs and glancing up at the counter as if we couldn't believe how long it was taking for our food. It killed me, both of us sitting there not talking. I didn't know why it was so important to me, but I didn't want Jake to know her better than me. I didn't want her to like him better.

"I'm going to see my dad," I blurted suddenly.

She looked at me, raising her eyebrows. "Oh yeah?"

"Yeah. He lives there. In Denver."

"Okay."

I swallowed. "I haven't seen him in a long time. He doesn't know I'm coming. I thought—I thought I would surprise him."

"Oh. I bet that'll make him happy."

I nodded. "Yeah. I think it will. I think he'll be happy about it."

She nodded, I nodded, and then we were back to sitting in thumb-twiddling silence. I really thought it would have made a difference, me telling her something personal like that, and I couldn't understand why it didn't. I expected us to just open up and tell each other all this innermost secret stuff about ourselves, and suddenly we'd be new best friends.

Then I realized I had killed the conversation again, but this time by lying. I didn't lie like Jake did, about stuff that didn't matter. I lied because I didn't tell her how I was really feeling. I didn't tell her that, yeah, maybe Dad would be happy to see me, but maybe he was going to be mad. I didn't tell her that I was afraid he might not even recognize me.

I was trying to stir up enough courage to say all this when Jake came sauntering back to the table, joining us with an insightful comment about what a relief it was to take a good dump. Then our food arrived, we scarfed it down, and a half hour later we were back on the road, all of us still working on the extra-large soft drinks.

And of course, Jake rode shotgun. I was going to say something to him about it being my turn, but it never seemed the right time.

In less than five minutes, we were out of Burns and back in open country, passing through desert lands even more empty than the ones before. If you took away the few bits of sagebrush, we could have been on the moon. To pass the time, I did some sketches, first of cows and scarecrows, then I started one of Anju. I could have worked on Dad's, but I was afraid I might finish it, and I didn't want to finish it, not yet.

They talked a little at first. Jake kept trying to get a conversation going, but each time it ended faster, after a while she didn't even nod or say "yeah," until finally Jake gave up and stared out the window. Drawing her, I was watching her face closely, and I could see what Jake meant. She looked sad most of the time, but sometimes she got this look of total and utter despair, as if she was going to burst out crying or screaming because she couldn't take it anymore. It lasted only a second, and I never would have believed I could see all that on her face in that short amount of time, but it really was there.

It rained once, a total downpour that lasted maybe ten minutes, big golf ball raindrops pounding on the roof. Nothing like what we got in Rexton, where it was just weenie drizzle that lasted for hours at a time. This storm let us have it all at once. Anju slowed the car to walking speed, and I thought, My God, it will take an eternity to get to Boise, but then it was over as fast as it started.

We stopped once so Jake could take a leak—which he did right there on the side of the road, barely even bothering to turn his back—but otherwise we just rifled over the gentle hills, passing through both Vale and Ontario in a blur of dust, soon joining up with Interstate 84. I barely noticed when we crossed out of Oregon into Idaho. So far, it was the same wasteland as what we'd just been seeing.

I finished the picture of Anju, then decided to close my eyes for just a second to rest them, but I must have fallen asleep, because I woke when the car stopped and found we were waiting at a traffic light in downtown Boise. It was a wide four-lane road with a pristine park on the right; the domed capitol and some other moderately large buildings were up ahead.

The road was slick with rain, but the sky was clear. A low mountain range that was more like a series of tall hills loomed behind the buildings, smooth and free of trees, a bit of snow cresting the rounded peaks. Anju drove through a downtown area that reminded me of Rexton, big without being big-city big, and pointed at a gray monolithic building that was at least ten stories high.

"That's where I work," she said.

"Yeah?" Jake said. "Bet you're president."

"I work in the deli in the basement."

"Oh," Jake said. "Well . . . I bet you get lots of free sandwiches."

She shrugged. "It pays the rent."

She lived a couple of miles from the capitol, in an old house that had been converted into six apartments. A green Chevette up on blocks, without wheels, was parked out front. A couple of teenagers in faded denim sat on the wooden steps of the house across the street. Anju led us inside, down a dark, narrow hall that smelled like mildew. Hers was the last of three doors.

"Well," she said, leading us inside, "it's not much, but it's mine."

Like she said, it wasn't much—a tiny living room, half of which was taken up by a brick fireplace, an alleylike kitchen with a green linoleum floor, and what I at first thought was a closet in the back but turned out to be her bedroom. She had done the best she could with the place, decorating with pots of dried flowers and Van Gogh prints. Anju went to an end table by the fireplace and looked at an answering machine next to a neon-pink phone. She looked at it a long time, and I saw that dark shadow pass over her face again, before she finally turned back to us.

"You're welcome to crash here for the night," she said. "Unless you have to get going. Either way. If you want me to drop you off somewhere, I can do that, too. You know, whatever."

Jake wanted to stay, and I was more of the mind to get going, so we decided to call Greyhound to see when the next bus was to Denver. Jake said he'd rather ride Amtrak if he had to ride anything, but Anju told us there was no Amtrak train service in Boise, just a bus that connected with Amtrak trains. It turned out that the next bus left at ten forty-five, and just to get to Salt Lake City would take over seven hours. There was another bus at eleven in the morning. Jake said we should wait for that one and that, who knows, maybe we'd find a ride before then that would get us there faster. I didn't want to drag out the trip too long, but spending a little more time with Anju didn't seem that bad.

We ordered a pizza from a place that Anju said was real good and Jake insisted on paying for it. While we gobbled our Meatlover's Delight, we shot the breeze about life in Boise, which Anju said was about as boring as a place could be.

"Well, why don't you move, then?" Jake said, wiping pizza sauce off his chin with a napkin. "You could go anywhere."

Before she could answer, the person in the next apartment turned on his stereo and blasted his music, the bass turned up so high I felt the vibrations even through the floor. Anju put down her paper plate and banged on the wall three times, hard. A few seconds later, the music's volume dropped.

"Guy's an idiot," Anju said.

"You didn't answer my question," Jake said.

She shrugged. "I don't know. Just no reason to go anywhere else, I guess."

"Did you grow up here?" Jake said.

She took a bite of her pizza. "Moobed 'ere," she mumbled.

"Why?"

She frowned. "What is this, the Spanish Inquisition?"

"Nobody expects the Spanish Inquisition!" I exclaimed.

I saw it as my chance to join in, but once again I felt like an idiot when they both gave me confused looks.

"From *Monty Python*," I said.

"Oh right," Anju said. "I had some friends into that."

"Dude," Jake said, "that's so old. Nobody our age watches that stuff."

I thought he was wrong, that people our age did watch *Monty Python*, but without other people our age around to ask, I didn't see any way to prove my point. Instead I just shrugged and went back to eating my pizza, hoping that the warmth I felt on my face was from the pizza and not from blushing.

"Anyway," Jake said, "I was just curious why you moved here."

We had to wait while she took her time chewing, but finally she just shrugged again—she was doing a lot of shrugging—and said, "Came up with John."

"John?" Jake said. "Was that—?"

"Same guy."

"Oh."

"We came up from Salt Lake City," she went on. "I met him in high school. Freshman year, actually. I wouldn't go out with him at first, but he kept asking. Then we were together all the time . . . I really thought we were going to be together forever, back then."

Looking at Jake, I could see that he hadn't expected the conversation to veer in this direction. Anju's eyes became distant, her shoulders dropped, and she bowed her head, as if her whole body was collapsing.

"A lot of Mormons down there in Utah," he said, obviously trying to change the subject.

"Yeah," Anju said. "John was Mormon."

"Oh," Jake said.

"It's why we moved up here," Anju said. "His parents didn't want us to be together unless I converted. My mother didn't want us to be together unless he converted to Catholic. So instead John just asks me to marry him at the senior prom and said we should just move away and start our own life. Love was all that mattered anyway. That's what he said." She was quiet a long time, and I was hoping that was it, she'd gotten it out of her system, but then she shook her head and sighed. "I guess I was wrong."

"Oh," Jake said, "well, people change."

She didn't respond, and it was such a lame comment on his part that I felt like I had to jump in and change the subject.

"Hey, how's your mom?" I said.

I knew as soon as I said it that my comment was even more lame than his, but there was no taking it back. Jake looked at me as if I was the world's number 1 moron, and it didn't make me feel any better when Anju's expression grew even darker.

"I don't know," she said.

"Oh," I said. "Sore subject. Sorry I—"

"She told me when I was packing my things that if I moved away with John that I was no longer her daughter."

"Ouch," Jake said.

"Yeah. I sent her a Christmas card the first year. She sent back a white envelope a few days later. I thought, Great, we're getting somewhere. When I opened the envelope, all I found was my card—torn up into dozens of tiny pieces."

"Double ouch," Jake said.

"Really one of those Hallmark moments, huh?" She had that bleak look again, the one that made her face look like a skull, and there was no way I was saying something stupid just to break the tension. "Yeah," she said again. "Yeah, anyway, water under the bridge. Just moving on, you know. Best thing."

We ate quietly for a while, then Jake made some stupid comment about how you just can't find good pizza anymore, and that got the conversation going again. We ate, we talked, and the night drew on, with Anju getting more and more withdrawn. All that talk about Anju's mother made me think about my mom again, and it started to gnaw on me that I should call her. It'd been only a day, but I didn't want her doing anything crazy. I didn't want to seem like a wuss in front of Anju, but I didn't want my face to end up on the back of a milk carton either.

"Hey, can I use your phone?" I asked Anju.

"Sure," she said. "Who you want to call?"

"Oh, just, um, you know—check in at home. Let them know I'm okay and that sort of thing." After learning about Anju's situation with her mom, I didn't want to specifically say *Mom*, thinking that might make her feel bad.

"He probably just wants to call one of his girlfriends," Jake said quickly. "He's probably got one here in Boise. Charlie's got them all over. Love 'em and leave 'em, that's his motto."

I ignored him. "It'd be long distance. I hope that's okay. It'd just be for a minute."

"No problem," she said. "You can take the phone into my room so you can have some privacy. Just ignore the mess."

The neon-pink phone next to the answering machine was a cordless, and I picked it up on my way to her room. The whole apartment was so small, and the door to her room so thin, that I didn't think closing the door would provide a lot of privacy, but I did it anyway. All she had in the room was a narrow bed and a four-drawer dresser, but even so I still had to practically sit on the bed to close the door. Clothes were piled all over the floor and the dresser, and the room had a slight musty odor. The blinds were mostly closed, and the room was dim except for a spot on the bed where bars of horizontal shadows from the blinds fell on the hot pink bedspread.

Nobody answered, so I left a message saying I was all right and not to worry and that sort of thing. I told her I'd call again soon. I wondered where she was. Maybe she was out shopping. It made me feel lousy.

Hanging up the phone, I noticed a little blue spiral notebook sticking out from under the bed.

I had no business picking it up. It was a total invasion of her privacy. But the corner of the notebook was worn and wrinkled, as if it had been heavily used, and there were doodles all over it. I wondered if she was an artist. I decided to take just a quick peek.

I picked it up and flipped through the pages. Right away, my heart started to pound and my palms sweat.

It wasn't a drawing pad.

It was a journal.

There *were* doodles in the margins on some pages, but mostly the journal was full of her meticulous blue handwriting, the writing so tiny I had to lift it close to read it. Most of the entries in the beginning were short, and the spelling sometimes creative. *Jan 8—Went to the Mall with John and we both bot new clothz.* But as I quickly flipped through it, the entries got longer, and they were more personal, about how John was acting funny, about how they were fighting a lot, and then, after he left, long, rambling entries about how she missed him and how her whole life was going to hell. I was mostly scanning, but I caught phrases like *hate myself* and *life sucks so much.*

It was the last entry in the book, though, that made me stop dead. She started off ranting about John and how she hated him but was still in love with him, making hardly any sense. It wasn't much different from some of the previous entries, except for the last line before all those empty white pages:

I Think maybee I'll just take the gun and kill Myself like I plannd.

chapter twelve

I reread that last sentence again and again, trying to understand if I was misunderstanding somehow. Kill herself? She couldn't really mean what she was saying. She was down, but she just didn't seem the type. Of course, I didn't really know what *type* a truly suicidal person was, but I figured you'd just be able to tell. I mean, I'd thought about it from time to time too, but only in the most distant way, like wondering how everyone would feel when I was gone. I'd never actually made plans to do it. No matter how bad my life got, there was the whole pain thing that went hand in hand with suicide I just couldn't get past.

If I'd had more time, I would have read some of the last couple entries in more detail, but then I heard footsteps in the living room. They sounded as if they were approaching, so I snapped the notebook closed and shoved it under the bed, leaping toward the door all in one motion.

I opened the door. Anju, however, had already passed and was heading to the kitchen. She glanced over her shoulder.

"Oh hey," she said. "I'm getting some water for Jake and me. You want some?"

"Um, sure," I said. My heart felt as if it was going to leap right out of my throat.

"So how's life back on the funny farm?" Jake asked from the couch.

He was lying on the couch, eyes closed and hands behind his head, and I was glad for it. If he was looking at me, he might have seen something funny on my face, which probably would have made him say something stupid. I made my way back to the living area, taking a seat on the floor. Anju brought us our water, and we made small talk for a little while longer. Apparently they had been talking about how *American Idol* was what was wrong with television these days.

I tried to join in, but all I could think about was that journal, so I kept losing track of the conversation. At one point, Anju asked if I was feeling all right, and I told her it was just my stomach, pizza didn't always agree with me. Soon the conversation died, and after a few minutes of us just listening to the faint pulsing of the neighbor's stereo, Anju got up and stretched her arms.

"Well," she said, "I think I'm going to take a shower and then head off to bed. I know it's early, but all the driving wiped me out. I know I'm being a bad host."

"No, you're great," I said, with so much enthusiasm that they both looked at me funny. I couldn't help it: I was afraid that as soon as she was behind that closed door, she was going to off herself. "Maybe we can do breakfast in the morning," I added.

"Maybe," Anju said. "I have to get to work pretty early, though. You guys are welcome to stay here until you have to catch your bus."

We both thanked her for all her generosity, and then she wandered off to the bathroom, rubbing her eyes and yawning. I wanted to say something to her, but I couldn't think of anything but *Hey, don't kill yourself, okay?* And I just didn't see how that would help much. As soon as the bathroom door closed, though, I leaned over to Jake and whispered to him about what I'd read in the journal. He'd looked about ready to fall asleep, but as soon as my words registered, he sat up and stared at me.

"You serious?" he said.

"Why would I joke about a thing like that?" I said.

"I don't know, I just . . ." He shook his head. "Man, what a thing to do. And all over some stupid guy."

"You think she means it?"

"Who knows. Maybe. Yeah, probably. I told you something seemed wrong about her."

"Yeah, but . . . suicide? It's so . . ." I couldn't think of the word. It was then that we heard the shower start up in the bathroom. Water gurgled behind the walls, the pipes moaning and creaking.

Jake looked at me, then stood and headed for her room.

"What are you doing?" I said.

"I'm going to look for the you-know-what," he said.

"The journal?"

"Not the journal. The other thing." He was almost to her door.

"Jake, you can't do this."

"Why not? If we just take the gun, she won't be able to go through with it."

I started after him. "You can't just *take* it!"

He was in her room now, opening her drawers, searching through the clothes. I watched from the doorway. The shower was still running.

"This is wrong," I said.

"It's wrong to stop somebody from blowing their brains out?" Jake said.

"What happens when she notices it's gone?" I said.

"Hopefully, by then we'll be gone."

Having found no gun in the dresser or the end table, he was now looking under the bed. He picked up the notebook, flipped through it quickly, then put it back. He looked through shoe boxes and found nothing but shoes. Finally, he pulled out a green gym bag. At first it seemed it was full of actual gym clothes, but then he pulled out a small black revolver that had been wrapped in her socks.

"Bingo," he said.

"Oh man," I said. I had been hoping she hadn't literally meant what she had written, but now it was obvious she had. Suddenly I regretted all that pizza I had eaten. My stomach was doing flip-flops.

The shower stopped. We darted back to the living area. Jake spotted my backpack and shoved the gun inside.

"What're you doing?" I demanded.

"It's the best place to hide it," he said.

"I'm not keeping that thing in there! What if—what if it goes off?"

"The safety's on."

"Oh, and I suppose you know all about guns?"

"A little," he said. "My dad—"

The bathroom door clicked open, steam pouring into the hall. Jake zipped the bag and tossed it onto the couch. I flinched, expecting the gun to go off, but the bag just landed with a thump. Anju, wearing a white terrycloth robe, stepped into the hall. She was drying her hair with a white towel, and when she saw us, she stopped. I realized we must have made quite the picture, the two of just standing there frozen in place, neither of us saying a word.

"Something wrong?" she asked.

"No," I said.

"We were just talking," Jake explained. "You know, about stuff. Guy stuff. You'd think it's stupid."

"Ah," she said. "Well, good night."

We told her good night, both of us practically shouting, and then she disappeared behind her bedroom door.

"This is so wrong," I said.

"Shh," Jake said.

I took a step closer to him, dropping my voice even lower. "What are we going to do, just leave with it?"

"That's the plan."

"And take it with us, on the bus and everything?"

He crossed his arms and stared at me. "You got a better idea?"

But I didn't get a chance to answer. Anju's bedroom door flew open, and she marched out, now wearing purple pajama bottoms and a Snoopy T-shirt, her hair loose and still glistening. She looked like a Doberman ready to pounce. A small one, maybe, but just as mean.

"Where is it?" she said.

"Where's what?" Jake asked, playing the part of Tweedledumb.

She held out her hand. "Give it back."

"I don't know what you're—"

"GIVE IT BACK!"

Jake flinched. I probably flinched too. You didn't expect such a loud noise to come out of a person so small. She could have spoken to a twenty thousand—seat stadium without a megaphone with that kind of volume. I started toward the backpack.

"Don't, Charlie," Jake said.

Anju, though, saw where I was headed. Jake beat her to it, holding it away from her, using his other hand to hold her back. She tried desperately to get the bag, clawing at it like some kind of animal, but Jake had no trouble keeping it away from her.

"Why are you doing this?" she cried.

"I read your journal," I said.

I don't know what made me say it. Maybe it was her face: It had the fierce, savage look of a starving person grappling for a piece of meat. It made her look terrible, and afraid, and pitiful, and I didn't want her to go on looking that way. All the fight went out of her immediately. She no longer looked angry. She looked like she wished she was somewhere else.

"You had no—" she began, and then had to stop and swallow. "You had no right to do that."

"I know," I said. "I'm sorry."

"We just don't want you to do anything stupid," Jake said.

"I'm not—I mean, I don't . . ." She sighed. "Please just give it back to me. It's just for self-protection."

"We'll just keep it for a while," Jake said. "We'll mail back to you later."

"That's just stuff I write!" she cried. "It doesn't mean anything. I just—I just use it as a way to vent. I wouldn't really do that!"

Neither of us said anything.

"Come on!" she said.

"A couple months," Jake said. "I promise."

Anju didn't move, but I'd never seen someone's face turn red so fast. It was as if Jake had lit her on fire. She pointed at the door.

"Out!" she said.

"What?" Jake said.

"Out! *Now!*"

Just like that, we were hustled into the hall. She slammed the door hard enough to bring dust raining down from the ceiling. Both of us were too stunned to move. After a moment, I heard Anju's muffled crying. Jake made a motion to knock on the door, then let his arm fall slack. He turned and headed for the outside door. I stopped him, reached into the bag, and took out my drawing pad. I ripped out the picture of Anju and slid it under her door. I didn't know what she'd think of it, but I hoped she'd see it as an apology. I hoped she'd see it as a sign that somebody had taken the time to really look at her.

I followed Jake outside and found him standing on the sidewalk. The night was cool, the street quiet. One of the street lamps down the way made a buzzing sound like someone humming.

"What now?" I asked.

He shrugged. "I guess we go catch that bus."

It was already half past nine by the time we got booted from Anju's place. We had no idea where the station was, but we found a phone booth a couple of blocks away, and there was a map of the city in the middle of the phone book. We were in luck. The station was a little over a mile away.

Hoofing it through the dark streets, we argued about the gun. I wanted to throw it into the nearest trash can, or drop it down a sewer grate, but Jake wouldn't have any of it. He said it belonged to Anju and he'd send it back to her when she was in a better state of mind, just as we'd promised.

"They'll never let us take it on the bus," I insisted. I was already breathing heavily, and struggling to keep up with Jake's near-jogging pace. What I really should have thrown away were all those textbooks, but there was no way I was going to do that.

"Oh, they don't even check your bags on the bus," Jake replied. "We could probably take on a bazooka in a telescope bag and nobody would stop us."

"Well, you're taking the bag," I said. "No way I'm getting caught with it."

"Fine by me."

The station was easy enough to find, marked with a big lighted sign that read, BUS. The front was all glass, and I saw a half-dozen people sitting inside on the red plastic seats. A bank clock down the street showed that it was just after ten o'clock. After forking out nearly ninety bucks for two tickets to Salt Lake City (Jake didn't want to buy tickets all the way to Denver, insisting we could find another way to get there), we spent the next forty-five minutes hanging out in a lobby that smelled like the underside of a bridge. None of the people waiting looked like they spoke English, and only a few looked like they bathed on a regular basis. When a driver in a blue uniform came through the double doors and told us our bus was ready to board, I handed the backpack to Jake.

Turned out Jake was right. When we climbed into the bus, we handed the driver our tickets and he didn't even glance at the backpack. Jake smiled smugly, but I still didn't start to relax until the bus pulled away from the station. Even then, I still hated that we had the gun with us.

chapter thirteen

Except for a couple quick stops in little towns whose names I quickly forgot, where the bus picked up a few wayward passengers each more alien-looking than the last, it was a long drive down I-84. I didn't think I was going to sleep, but somewhere around the Idaho border I dozed off and didn't wake again until we pulled into the terminal in Salt Lake City. My neck actually made a cracking sound when I turned my head, alarming me. If I kept this up, I'd be wearing a neck brace before too long.

The early morning sun filled the bus with pale orange light. Jake, already awake, smiled at me. My backpack sat on his lap. Judging by the way he turned away from me when I said good morning, I assumed my breath smelled like a gym locker.

It was barely seven o'clock, but there was already a buzz of traffic coming from the nearby overpasses. What I assumed were the Rocky Mountains loomed over the city; thin vaporous clouds clung to the tops of the peaks. These mountains weren't anything like the Cascades back at home, which you often couldn't see unless you were right on top of them. The Rockies were always there, towering over everything, making all the human activity seem like nothing more than the scurrying of lots of ants.

The terminal was huge compared to the one back in Boise, as big as some airports. After we both hit the restroom, I asked Jake if he wanted to get something to eat, and he said sure. We wandered down the huge six-lane West 400th and found a Denny's-type place a couple of blocks away, near Pioneer Park.

I got the French toast. Jake got waffles with strawberries. I kept the backpack on the seat next to me, and I found myself glancing at it from time to time.

"Will you relax," Jake said, wiping whipped cream off his chin with a napkin.

"We could sell it at a pawnshop," I said.

"No."

"It might go off."

"It won't."

I finally realized that no matter how much I argued, he wasn't changing his mind, so I changed the subject. "How do you want to get to Denver?" I asked. "I saw that the Amtrak station is in the same place as the bus depot. You want to ride a train instead?" I was eager to get going. It was now Wednesday, and I was starting to worry about how much school I was missing. It was a pretty stupid thing to worry about, but I hated getting too far behind on my homework.

"Yeah, sure," he said. "But there's something I think we should do first."

"What's that?"

He took a gulp from his Coke before answering. I couldn't believe he was drinking Coke for breakfast. There should be a law that you can't drink Coke in the morning. "Go see Anju's mom," he said.

"What?"

"Dellinger can't be that common," Jake said matter-of-factly, as if he hadn't noticed the surprise in my voice. "It can't be hard to find her."

"How do you know her last name's Dellinger?"

"Because I saw the nameplate next to the front door, dummy."

"Oh. But why? You want to give her the you-know-what? Is that what you're thinking?

"No, no."

I shook my head. "Then I don't—"

"I want to try to patch things up between her and Anju. Somebody should do it."

I couldn't believe it. We were hundreds of miles away from home, and he wanted to go play psychologist. I kept trying to convince him that we didn't have time, that his idea would probably only make things worse, but nothing I said changed his mind. After breakfast, he stopped at the phone booth out in the lobby. There were six Dellingers in the book.

Despite my protests that it was way too early to call, he used the change he'd gotten paying for breakfast to start working his way down the list. He struck gold with the third one, listed as an M. Dellinger. He'd been asking all of them if they had a daughter named Anju, and I watched Jake for the usual look of disappointment. But this time he stood up a little straighter.

"No," he said, "she's still alive. We were just talking to her yesterday in Boise. I was wondering—"

The woman on the other end said something.

"Yes," Jake said, "I understand, but . . . ma'am? Ma'am, are you there?" He looked at me. "She hung up."

"Big shock," I said.

"She told me that if Anju's not dead, she might as well be."

"Ouch."

"This might be tougher than I thought."

I shook my head. "I hate to tell you I told you so."

"No you don't."

"Okay," I said, "I don't. Ready to give up?"

"Not a chance."

Then he was back on the phone again, calling one of the local cab companies. Fifteen minutes later, a green cab pulled up to the curb and we hopped inside. Jake now had the gun in his inside jacket pocket, wrapped in some paper towels to hide its general shape. Because I'd whined so much about having it in my backpack, Jake had taken my pack into the restroom while we waited for the cab and made the switch. It made me feel a little better, but not much.

After a short cab ride through the guts of the city, we passed through the slumbering campus of Westminster College and stopped at an apartment complex a few blocks away. It was an older building, two stories and maybe ten units, but nicely maintained. Sprinklers were running on the lawn. Jake paid the cabbie and asked him to wait, saying it was just a quick errand.

"You're just going to go knock on the door," I said.

"Sure," Jake said.

She lived on the bottom floor, the last unit on the end. Jake had to ring the doorbell three times before we finally heard the click of the dead bolt. The door opened a crack and a middle-aged woman with red hair that bordered on purple looked at us over the gold safety chain. There was no doubt we had the right woman:

She was obviously Filipino or something similar, and she looked a lot like Anju, just with deeper facial grooves. I saw the top of her white terrycloth robe. I thought it was interesting that she was wearing the same robe as her daughter.

"What you want?" she said. Anju had no accent to speak of, but this woman had one so thick it almost didn't sound like English.

"I'm the one who called," Jake said. "About Anju."

The woman started to close the door, and Jake stopped it with his hand.

"Wait a minute," Jake said.

"I scream you not let go!" the woman protested.

"Fine, scream," Jake said. "I just thought you might want to talk to Anju before she kills herself."

It was enough to cause the woman to thaw, if only a little. "You say this to trick me?"

"No, ma'am," Jake said. "We're real worried about her."

She nodded, looking at the ground. Then she closed the door and Jake didn't stop her. I thought that might be it, she'd washed her hands of us, but then she opened the door and motioned us inside.

The apartment was at least three times as big as Anju's, but it seemed much smaller because of all the expensive furniture crammed into it. The woman introduced herself as Malaya and had us sit on a plush white couch that looked like it belonged in the lobby of a Hilton. A giant crucifix, with Jesus on the cross in gory bloody detail, was mounted above the mantle of a white brick fireplace, a mantle covered with dozens of smaller crucifixes.

A fluffy Persian cat that was just as white wandered into the room and hopped up on the arm of the love seat, where Malaya had just taken a seat. There was a strong odor in the room that reminded me of gasoline, a smell that hit me right when we walked inside, and I couldn't figure out what it was until I realized it was the woman's perfume.

Without waiting to be asked, Jake launched into what was going on with Anju. He didn't hold anything back, telling her how John had left and how depressed that had made Anju, how she had gone to Bend looking for him only to find that he had already found another woman, and how we read her journal and discovered that she planned to kill herself. He finished by saying how sad Anju seemed that she and her mother hadn't been able to patch things up. I thought he laid that part on a little thick, but I could see what he was trying to do.

Up until this point, Malaya stroked her purring cat and looked at the carpet between us, a blank expression on her face, but finally, when Jake spoke about the mother and daughter's strained relationship, I saw something give in her face, like a dam straining to hold back a rising river. She closed her eyes, seemed to gather herself, then looked up at us defiantly.

"Her fault," she said. "She left. Her fault."

Jake didn't say anything for a while, and we sat there listening to the cat purr. I thought Jake had done all he could, that there were no more cards to play. But Jake continued to sit there, not saying anything, as if he was waiting for something to happen. Then I realized he was trying to wait out Malaya, and finally he succeeded.

"She could call," she said. "She could come home. Lots she could do. I still here. I never leave."

Jake nodded slowly. "That's true," he said. "And she might. But you know, she might not. And do you really want the last thing your daughter remembers about you to be how you tore up the Christmas card she sent you?"

I cringed, expecting an explosion. There was a flash of anger on Malaya's face, but it was only there for a moment, and then the dam finally broke. She didn't move, and she didn't sob, but tears rolled down her face. She blinked furiously. She made me think of a porcelain doll that had miraculously shed tears.

"I make crazy sometimes," she said. "I know. I wish I didn't."

"We all make crazy sometimes," Jake said. "But you get a second chance. You can call her."

Mayala shook her head.

"She sent you the card," Jake said. "That was her attempt. Now it's your turn."

"She no talk to me."

"How do you know unless you try?"

Mayala was silent for a while. "You know her papa kill himself?"

This was news to both Jake and me, and we exchanged looks.

"No," Jake said, "we didn't."

"He was in war. Vietnam. Lots of bad memories. He got very depressed. Sometimes happy, but most of the time depressed. Sometimes very, very depressed, never get out of bed some days. Lots of times he try kill himself. Finally, he use gun."

"I'm sorry," Jake said. "But now you have a chance to stop Anju from making the same mistake. You can call her."

"When?"

"Now," Jake said.

Mayala was shaking her head, but Jake rose and went to the antique rotary phone on the end table and held up the receiver. Mayala bowed her head, and for a long time I thought she was going to just sit there, but finally she rose and made her way over to it. He handed her the phone and she stared at it as if it was an alien thing. Finally, with great care, she dialed, and I could hear the clicks of the rotary across the room.

It was hard to hear the person on the other end clearly, but I heard a woman say hello. Mayala said nothing. The woman said hello again. Malaya looked at Jake, who nodded at her.

Mayala swallowed and closed her eyes. When she spoke, it was with a tiny voice. "Anju," she said.

There was a lot of crying on both ends of the line, but things seemed to go reasonably well. We sneaked out before they'd finished. The morning dew had burned off while we were inside, the sun much higher over the Rockies. The cab had abandoned us, so we started walking toward the Westminster campus, thinking we could catch a bus back into town from there. Jake lit up a cigarette. He didn't say much, but I could sense this warm smugness all around him that got annoying after only a few minutes.

"There's still no guarantee they'll work it out," I said.

"Nope," he said, blowing out smoke, "there's no guarantee."

"It's not like one phone call is going to make everything right."

"Probably not, but it's a start. It's also a good sign that Anju's mom didn't even have to look up the number."

I hadn't noticed that, and it made me irritated, Jake noticing something like that when I didn't. We walked on for a while saying nothing, people mowing their lawns around us, sprinklers gyrating.

"You know," I said, "she could always go out and buy another gun."

He stopped dead in his tracks. We were getting close to the campus, where the houses and the upscale condominiums had been replaced by cheaper apartments, bicycles parked on the patios, Westminster College placards in many windows.

"What is it with you?" he said.

"Huh?"

"You want Anju to kill herself or something?"

"No, of course not!"

He dropped his cigarette on the sidewalk and ground it out with his shoe. "Then why are you so negative?"

"I'm not negative."

"Yes, you are," Jake insisted. "It's like you wanted me to fail here."

"I didn't—" I began.

"You think it's better to do nothing? Is that what you think? We should just sit by and let her blow her brains out without even trying?"

"No!" I replied.

"You can't always do nothing, Charlie. You can't always just sit on your hands and wait for things to take care of themselves.

Sometimes you got to *try*. At least try. Jesus. I mean, Anju might have *died*. Don't you get that?"

"I understand, but—"

"But what? This isn't high school. This isn't like sitting in class hoping the teacher doesn't call on you. This is real life. Things you do matter. I may not get good grades or anything like you, and maybe I'm going to flunk out of high school, but high school's pretend, Charlie. It's pretend. This is real. You can't live in a pretend world forever."

"I know that!" I shouted.

"Good!"

"Fine!"

We walked the rest of the way to campus, both of us sulking, me lingering a little behind him. I was mad, but I was mostly mad at myself. He was right. For some reason, I had wanted him to fail, and it made me feel very small. I'd always thought of myself as so much better than him in so many ways. Yeah, he may have been cool, and he may have known how to talk to girls, but he was a flunky who was going to end up pumping gas while I raked in the big money as a doctor. But he had made me realize how shallow this thinking was. I'd always thought of myself as above the preppies, that I wasn't fake like they were, but now I seemed just as fake as them.

Jake had done something *real*. He had made a difference in somebody's life. What had I ever done, except hide in my little shell, hoping nobody would pick on me?

It wasn't until we were riding the bus back into town that we were finally talking again. At first, it was just inane comments about all the Mormons, how everyone we saw on the street was somebody's cousin, comments that got some harsh glares from the other passengers. There was still something there between us, something unsettled, but it was like we'd called a truce. We transferred buses a couple of times, finally getting off right at the bus and train depot. I started for the door, but stopped when I realized Jake wasn't with me.

He stood on the sidewalk, grinning like a mad monkey.

"What?" I said.

"Let's go have some fun," he said.

"Huh?"

He decided to show me rather than tell me. There was a big store down the road called Price-N-Pride, full of mostly Wal-Mart—type stuff, and toward the back of the sterile air-conditioned aisles, he found a large package of brightly colored latex balloons. He held them up to his smirking face.

"You got to be kidding," I said.

"I think it's time for the Water Balloon Boys to ride again," he said.

"No way."

"Aw, where's your sense of adventure?"

"This isn't even our city!"

He nodded. "All the better. We get them wet, and then we ride for the hills."

"You're crazy!"

He laughed like a maniac and headed for the checkout register, picking up a cheap blue duffle bag along the way. Nothing I said could change his mind. Outside, he pointed to the tallest building in the area, a big gray hunk of concrete at least ten stories high. I told him traffic was too busy and that we might cause accidents. He called me a wuss, but didn't press on with the idea either. Instead he said we should target the nicest-dressed people on the street and give them a little wet surprise. I told him we'd probably get arrested, and he replied with more laughter.

Using the public bathroom at Pioneer Park, we filled up as many water balloons as his blue duffle bag would hold—at least a dozen. The water sloshed inside the bag as Jake carried it. I wore my backpack on my back. He wanted to put balloons in there, too, but I wouldn't let him. No way I was letting my drawings get soaked. Jake agreed that this was probably not a good idea and even stuck his wad of money down at the bottom of the bag, beneath the American History text. He said if he was caught and I wasn't, then at least I'd have the cash.

"I can't believe we're doing this," I said.

"Who should we target first?" he said.

"Nobody."

"Aww."

"Jake, this is nuts."

"Afraid you're going to get caught?"

"Well yeah! Yeah, I am!"

He took a seat on a park bench. Traffic on West 300th grumbled by, buses spewing out diesel exhaust, brakes squealing. Men in suits, women in nice dresses, mothers holding the hands of children—all of them walked by on the sidewalks, and I felt sorry for all of them. None of them had any idea that they might be soaking wet in a few minutes.

"Look at it this way," Jake said, "all these people—they want to get wet. They just can't admit it to themselves. Look at them, Charlie. Just walking along, safe in their little worlds. They have no excitement in their lives. We're going to give them some excitement. We're going to shake things up for them. In the end, they'll thank us."

"I really have a hard time believing they're going to thank us for making them soaking wet," I said.

"Well, maybe not in so many words," he said, and he pulled out a yellow water balloon. "But inside, deep down, they really will be grateful."

A young guy in a pin-striped gray suit, a cell phone up to his ear, walked by our bench. Jake grinned at me. I had a vision of him grinning at me inside a prison cell. I was about to say something along the lines of *How do you feel about prison food?*, but then the water balloon was in the air. I watched the jiggling latex hurtling toward its unsuspecting victim, hoping that it would miss, hoping that if it did hit, it would hit only the man's ankles, but Jake's aim was too good. It hit the man right between the shoulder blades.

The man jerked to a stop. There was now a dark spot in the middle of his jacket, and water and bits of yellow balloon dribbling down his back.

"Gotcha!" Jake cried.

The guy turned. The astonishment on his face changed quickly to rage, a veil of red starting at his neck and extending all the way to his forehead.

"You little bastard!" the guy shouted, and started for Jake.

With a laugh, Jake ran. I had no choice but to follow him.

146

After a block, the guy gave up the chase. We rounded a corner and ducked into an alley, taking refuge behind a Dumpster, both of us breathing hard. It smelled like rotting fish. Jake looked at me and started laughing, and I couldn't help myself, I started laughing too.

"The look on that guy's face—" Jake wheezed.

"Priceless—" I gasped.

Jake laughed harder. "Like the commercial—"

"Yeah—"

And just like that, the Water Balloon Boys were back in business. The other end of the alley came out at a stoplight. We waited until a middle-aged guy pulled up in a convertible, a perky blond woman half his age in the passenger seat, and then both of us jumped out and lobbed water balloons right into their laps. We took off before the balloons even reached their targets, and we could still hear the woman screaming four blocks away.

Over the next half hour, we drenched two ladies in spandex jogging side by side, a group of balding old men in polo shirts, some gang-banger types on skateboards, and even a muscle-bound oaf on a motorized scooter who followed us for half a mile before we finally lost him inside a department store. In the store, we continued our act, heading into the men's restroom and hitting a guy standing at a urinal. He shrieked like a little girl. A beefy security guard tried to nab us on our way out, but we managed to slip by and scurry away.

We spaced out our attacks every few blocks, trying to avoid attracting too much attention, but eventually the inevitable happened. Jake hit the side of a tour bus with one of the balloons, and when it passed, there was a police car pulling up from the side street. The lights came on immediately.

"Run!" Jake cried.

I had no thought of giving up this time. We were the Water Balloon Boys, after all, a pair of nefarious criminals wanted all over the world, and to be caught by the law would mean certain hanging. It was run or die. So we ran, the pedestrians giving us a wide berth, the police siren screaming behind us. We ducked into an alley so narrow I could touch both brick walls with my elbows. I heard a screech of tires and, glancing over my shoulder, saw the police car stopped at the curb, two officers clambering out.

"Ho boy!" Jake cried.

The policemen yelled for us to stop. Jake dropped the bag of balloons and ran faster, me struggling to keep up. When we reached the street, he weaved around a guy on a bicycle and headed left. I followed, dodging a few pedestrians. There seemed nowhere to go but just on down the sidewalk. The policemen emerged from the alley, yelling at us. Jake may have been able to outrun them, but they were definitely gaining on me. Jake glanced over his shoulder at me, saw that he'd begun to stretch out a lead ahead of me, and slowed his pace to match mine.

"Go on!" I said.

"No way!" he replied.

He nodded toward a hotel. I didn't know what he meant until he ran that way, leaping over a cart of luggage and right through the revolving door. My legs feeling like they were going to collapse at any moment, I followed him into a plush lobby. There was a white stone fountain, green marble flooring, and a matching reception counter. A man behind the counter yelled at us, but we didn't stop, sprinting down a hall of doors and ducking into a stairwell. Jake went up one flight of stairs, me right behind him, and then down the red-carpeted hall, numbered doors on either side. One of the doors was open, a mop-and-broom cart parked right outside. A heavyset woman in a red uniform was backing her way out of the room.

"Oh thank you, ma'am," Jake said. "Dad sent us up here to get his wallet. Are you done?"

"Oh yes, yes," the woman said meekly, and stepped out of the way.

Jake smiled at her and we stepped inside, closing the door. It was just in time, because I heard the stairwell door down the hall open. A shout, running footsteps, the clank of elevator doors closing. Another heavy door opening at that end and more footsteps.

We waited for a good twenty minutes—each us taking turns mimicking the way people looked when they'd been hit by one of our balloons, stifling our snickers—then crept out into the hall like a pair of cat burglars. We took the stairs down to the main floor, then used an exit that led to a parking lot in the back, finally making our way through the busy streets to the depot. I was exhausted, but it was probably the best day I'd had in a long time. I couldn't even think of a close second, which said something about how lame my life had been.

It was now three o'clock in the afternoon, and the depot was bustling with activity, people carrying crying kids, businessmen pulling suitcases on wheels. There was a bus leaving for Denver in thirty minutes, but Jake insisted on going by train, and the next train wasn't for two hours.

"Enough time to get something to eat and maybe take a little nap," he said.

I'd forgotten we hadn't had lunch. After we bought our tickets and stuck them in the backpack, we had burgers at a greasy little cafeteria right there in the depot, then found an empty bench in the main lobby area. Jake rolled up his jean jacket and used it as a pillow, dozing off right away. I tried to do the same, using my backpack as a pillow, but my mind wouldn't relax. The high I'd been on from the water ballooning had finally started to fade, and now I was starting to think about Dad again.

We were getting closer.

We were definitely getting closer.

I was having a hard time remembering why I had ever thought seeing him was a good idea. I'd often said to myself that I should go see him, but I'd often said I should do lots of things and had never gotten around to them. What did I think was really going to happen? Did I really think giving him the portrait would change anything?

It was making me crazy thinking about it, so I decided to do some drawing, sketching the lobby area. It wasn't long before I felt some serious pressure down below, so I hopped up to go to the bathroom, slipping the pad underneath the backpack on the bench. Jake was snoring away. I thought about waking him to tell him where I was going, then decided he would be pretty angry at being woken up just because I was going to take a leak, so I let him sleep. It was a little decision, one I didn't think much about at the time, but it was going to change everything.

I was away for less than five minutes. When I was heading back to the bench, now feeling much more relaxed and maybe finally sleepy enough to take a nap, I saw the problem right away. And I was suddenly wide awake again.

My drawing pad was sitting there on the bench corner, but my backpack was gone.

chapter fourteen

"Stolen? What do you mean, stolen?"

Jake sat up, blinking away his sleep. Without his jacket to give him bulk, he looked thin and small in his rumpled T-shirt. I swallowed hard. All around us, people continued to walk purposefully to their destinations, hardly even giving us a glance, all of them oblivious to the crisis we now faced. The commotion in the lobby echoed off the tiled floor and the high ceilings. Outside the doors, a train screeched to a halt. I wondered if it was our train, then realized we still had at least an hour to go.

"I mean, it's gone," I said.

"You're joking," Jake said.

He was finally wide awake now, and the full impact of the situation seemed to finally hit him. If my backpack was stolen, that meant all our money was gone, as well as our tickets. He looked under the bench, then hopped up and began wandering around the terminal, searching next to vending machines and video games, as if the backpack was a pet that had just wandered off on its own. I watched him, waiting for him to understand what I had understood right away. The backpack was gone, and there was no getting it back.

Finally, he returned, looking pissed and miserable.

"How could this happen?" he said.

"I had to go to the bathroom."

"You should have woken me."

"I thought you'd be mad."

He gaped at me. "Mad? Don't you understand, Charlie? We have nothing now!"

I swallowed, remembering where the money had come from. "What are we going to do about the drug dealer? He's going to want his money."

"Oh, shut up!" he said. "I made up that stuff. The money was my foster dad's from when he sold his van."

"You made it up?"

"Yeah, so you'd go with me! God! What difference does it make now? We have nothing! *Nothing!*"

"They didn't get my drawing pad at least."

"Oh great!" he said with mock enthusiasm. "Because I'm sure they would have wanted that! They might have sold the drawings for a million dollars each!" He shook his head. "I mean, Jesus! You could have taken the backpack with you. That would have been the smart thing to do. What the hell were you thinking?"

"Well—"

He held up a hand. "Don't. Forget it. It doesn't matter. It's gone." It obviously mattered, a lot, but he kept repeating "it doesn't matter" as if he would eventually convince himself. Finally, he sighed. He reached into his pocket and pulled out a couple of twenties. He counted them. "Well . . . I didn't think I had enough on me, but I do. I have enough money for one ticket. You can still go to Denver. It's not a total loss."

"That's all right," I said.

"What?"

"I'm not going."

"Oh yes you are!"

I shook my head. "We should probably see this as a sign. I wasn't meant to go. It was a dumb idea to begin with."

"Charlie, come on. You're just getting scared 'cause you're going to see your dad soon. You don't want to chicken out now, when you're almost there."

"I'm not chickening out," I said. "I just don't want to do it anymore."

"Charlie—"

"I mean it, Jake. Why does it matter, anyway? I thought it did. I thought it would matter. But I don't have to see him. It's not like he's been there in my life, you know? It was just dumb, the whole thing. It's better if I don't go. At least I can pretend that maybe the picture might mean something to him. If I give it to him and he doesn't like it . . . it's just not worth it."

Jake started to say something, stopped, tried again, then turned away and muttered something.

"What was that?" I asked.

He looked at me. "I said you're full of crap."

"Okay, whatever," I said. "I'm just telling you how I feel."

"You may buy all that stuff, maybe you've convinced yourself, but the truth is that you're just a wuss."

I felt the tomato face coming on, a warmth that spread all the way to my ears. "Maybe it seems that way, but it really isn't. I've been thinking about it a lot, and I really don't see the point of going there."

"Nope," Jake said, "you're just a wuss."

I walked away. He followed me. I had known he was going to see it that way, that no amount of explaining would make him understand it was more than me just being a chicken.

"Wuss, wuss, wuss," he said.

"Oh, real mature," I said. I walked out of the terminal and onto the sidewalk, people streaming around me, the sun bright overhead. I didn't know where I was going. I just wanted to get away from him.

"I should have figured this would happen," he said.

I chose a random direction and started walking. "That's right, Jake, you should have."

"You're just a wuss right to the core."

I walked fast, but he stayed right next to me. I wouldn't look at him.

"That's right," I said. "You know everything, Jake. I'm just a chicken. There's nothing more to it than that."

"Just like with Jessa," he said.

It stopped me cold. I turned and stared at him. We stood next to a covered bus bench, where a grubby-looking wino in a gray trench coat was sleeping. I smelled the alcohol clinging to the guy even from where we stood.

"What?" I said.

He smirked a little and looked away, and just for a second, I thought he was going to say something else, maybe pretend he hadn't said it, but then he looked back at me and his face was set, his eyes hard.

"You wrote her that note, and then you chickened out."

"What are you talking about?" I said. "I put it in her locker, didn't I?"

"No, you didn't. You wrote it, but you didn't give it to her. Somebody else did."

"What are you . . ." I began, and then realized where he was going. The thought that someone else had given Tessa the note had never occurred to me, but now I realized that's exactly what had happened. "*You* did it?" I said, incredulous.

"That's right."

I felt like I'd been shot in the back. "Why?"

"Why? Because I knew you were too much of a wuss to give it to her."

"You took it from my notebook? You actually took it from my notebook?"

"No, no, no," he said. "I found it in the hall. You're just lucky it was me that found it and not someone else."

I couldn't believe what he was saying. Leo had almost killed me and he thought I was lucky? What would have been worse, broadcasting it on the news? Lying to me about the money was one thing, but this was the worst betrayal I could imagine. "I can't believe you did that to me," I said.

"Yeah, well, believe it. I was trying to help you."

"Help! Leo was going to rip off my face and feed it to his gerbils! How was that helping me?"

"Keep your voice down," Jake said.

I knew some of the people walking by were ogling us like we were animals in a zoo, but I didn't care. "I could have died!"

"You're exaggerating. You just needed that little nudge, and that's what I did. Just like I'm trying to do now. Stop you from wussing out. I know you want to give that portrait to your dad. So do it. No matter what happens, at least you can say you did it. That's something."

I was still reeling from what he had done to me, but all at once it came to me exactly why he had put that note in Tessa's locker, and it had nothing to do with me needing a nudge. He had needed a way to get me to go along with his crazy plan to travel halfway across the country, and what better way to do it than make Leo Gonzalez want to pulverize me. I didn't know exactly why it had been so important that I go with him when we hadn't spoken in years, but that must have been it. He wanted to go see his uncle, but he didn't want to do it alone.

"You did all this on purpose," I said.

"What?"

"To get me to go with you. Admit it. It wasn't about me at all. It was about you not wanting to take this trip alone. So you're the chicken. You're the wuss."

His eyebrows went up, and he tried to look confused, but there was just a little bit of a smirk, enough to make me think I'd nailed it right on the head and he was smiling because he was guilty.

"You're nuts," he said.

"I can't believe this!"

"Calm down. You're blowing things out of proportion. I really was trying to help you."

"Liar!" I said. My eyes felt watery, and I fought to keep the tears from spilling out. I would not cry in front of him. "You're a big fat liar!"

"I don't know why you're getting so upset about this."

It was hard to speak, and I was sputtering all over the words. "I thought you were my friend, Jake! That's why! But you turned out to be a jerk, just like everyone else."

"I am your friend, man. That's why I'm trying to get you to—"

"Oh yeah, then why didn't you ever admit you broke my Game Boy?"

I didn't think about the words first; they just came out. It took a moment for him to realize what I'd said, but I saw something change in his eyes. It was like they froze, like I was looking at a picture of him rather than the real person.

"I don't know what you mean," he said. "I told you back then, it was broke when I got it."

"That's crap." I probably should have stopped there, just let him have his little fantasy, but I couldn't. There was no way the Game Boy had been broken when I'd given it to him, because I had played with it just a few minutes before handing it to him. "That's why we can't ever be real friends, Jake," I said. "Friends don't lie. I thought maybe you'd changed, but you're still a liar."

I expected him to punch me. Maybe yell and scream and stomp his feet. Something violent. I knew I was taking my own life into my hands, that he could beat me in a fight without breaking a sweat, but I wanted to get a reaction out of him. I wanted to hurt him like he'd hurt me.

He didn't say anything for a long time, just stood there staring at me with those frozen eyes. I felt like all of Salt Lake City was watching, when really, nobody probably even noticed, except for the people on the streets who saw us as just obstacles in their paths. Maybe I had hurt him, maybe I hadn't, it was hard to tell, but he didn't get angry. He chewed on his bottom lip, nodded as if something had been decided, then took the money in his hand and stuffed it into my pocket. I was too stunned to stop him.

"Buy the ticket, Charlie," he said. "Give your dad the picture. Do it because then you can say you did."

Then he walked away. I watched him, thinking maybe he'd turn toward the station, but he walked right on past, rounded a corner, and was gone.

I don't know how long I stood there on the sidewalk, but it was a long time. I kept waiting for Jake to come back. No way he was going to just abandon me here in Salt Lake City, was he?

A bus grumbled by, spitting out black diesel clouds, and that snapped me back to reality. So I was on my own now. It was just me and my drawing pad, standing there on the sidewalk outside the depot, over five hundred miles from Oregon, eighty bucks in my pocket. I headed inside, planning on plunking it down on the counter and buying a ticket home. It was time to end this crazy road trip. Get back to getting good grades and making something of my life. Stop living in a fantasy. Stop worrying about a dad who didn't care whether I lived or died.

After waiting in line for a few minutes and finally making my way to the counter, I was ready to tell the clerk I wanted a ticket to Rexton. The clerk was an old man with white hair and a woolly white beard who made me think of Santa Claus.

"Destination?" he said.

I couldn't speak.

"Son?" he said.

The winter before Dad left, I had really wanted a new ten-speed bike for Christmas. I'd thought about it all year, but then the whole craziness between Mom and Dad had happened, and I had forgotten all about it. Now here was Santa Claus asking me how he could help me. Asking me what I wanted.

"I want a ticket to Denver," I said quickly.

Before I could change my mind, he'd taken my money and given me my ticket.

chapter fifteen

I don't remember much about the ride to Denver—the whole thing was like some kind of hazy dream, a rumble of foggy memories. I remember stepping onto the gray two-story train and handing my ticket to a black woman in a blue uniform. I remember the feel of the cloth coach seat and the garlic smell of the heavy greasy-haired man sitting next to me. I remember how the moon looked rising over the Rockies after the last of the crimson light had drained from the sky. But the memories are just fragments, and what I really remember clearly was waking to the screech of the train's brakes, and then the conductor telling us over the intercom that the local time in Denver was 6:15 a.m.

The train ride had lasted over fifteen hours, but it might as well have been fifteen minutes.

There was a great crush of people in the aisle, eager to get off the train, but I stayed seated, a swarm of butterflies making war in my stomach. So this was it. I was finally going to see Dad. If I just focused on giving him the portrait, maybe everything else would just take care of itself. That's what I told myself anyway.

Finally, after everyone else had disembarked, I stepped down the metal steps onto the concrete platform of Denver Union Station. The sky was a milky gray, the dawning sun invisible. Fog hung around the street-lamp lights, the air wet and cold. I followed a few straggler passengers into the old building, passed over the shiny tiled floors and through a handful of people shivering in the lobby and back outside. The station looked like it had been around since the 1800s, and I half expected an old stagecoach to be waiting outside, but it was just another big-city downtown, with a few cars, trucks, and a city bus or two passing along the street.

I turned right and walked along Wynkoop Street, in minutes finding myself in the middle of downtown Denver, the sidewalks quiet, everything closed except a couple of restaurants. I stopped at a phone booth and looked for the map of Denver inside, but someone had torn out that page. I walked a little farther and found a drugstore that was open, behind the counter a spindly red-haired guy who looked not much older than me. I knew Dad's address by heart because of the postcards he sent a few times a year, and I asked the guy how to get there.

"Oh yeah, that's the Cherry Creek area," he said. "Not too far. About five miles. Probably out by the country club."

He gave me the directions, drew me a little map on a napkin, and asked if I wanted to know which bus to take. I said sure, and he told me, but when I actually got outside I decided to walk. I knew I was just delaying things, but it was still early, and I didn't want to wake him. I didn't want to give him a reason to be mad right from the start.

It took me almost two hours to walk to the Cherry Creek area, most of it spent on Speer Boulevard, a busy commercial road. I watched the city come to life, the traffic picking up, the shopkeepers turning on their OPEN signs. The morning mist burned away, but the sky was still gray and the air crisp. When I reached the

Denver Country Club, I knew I was getting close. It was one of those fancy country clubs, with a golf course and tennis courts, out front a big building that looked like a hotel. I wondered if my dad was a member. I wondered if he was there right now.

That's when I stopped.

There was a green metal bench at the edge of the golf course, next to some leafless oak trees, and I took a seat. I don't know why I stopped. I told myself I was just going to catch my breath, since I'd walked a long ways, but I really wasn't that tired. And I sat there a lot longer than a few minutes. I knew Dad might be going to work, getting to his dentist's office to do all his dentist-type things, and that I might miss him if I didn't get going, but I sat there anyway. It may have been an hour. I watched some old guys in heavy parkas, who moved about as fast as turtles, making their way up the course. I watched other old guys come along to replace them.

Give your dad the picture. Do it because then you can say you did.

It was Jake's voice. And I realized, finally, that whether it made sense to give the portrait to Dad or not, that I was going to do it. I was going to do it so that I could say that I had done it. I'd come all this way, and once you'd come as far as I had, you couldn't just back out. What kind of story would that be, when people asked me what I did after we stole Mr. Harkin's Mustang? Once you'd gone down a road, you had to go all the way to the end or everything was a waste.

So I was walking again, much faster. Then running. Soon I was past the country club and into the posh homes of the Cherry Creek neighborhood, with houses that looked like they should have been on the covers of architecture magazines. I was breathing hard, sweat on my face, my shirt sticking to my back. I ran until my legs burned. Down one street, then the next, dogs barking, gardeners looking up from their hedges to stare at me.

Finally, I couldn't run anymore, and I collapsed against a birch tree at the corner of someone's yard, gasping for breath. I felt like I couldn't get enough air, and I wondered if it was the altitude. I'd heard they called Denver the Mile-High City.

When I looked up, I was there.

Dad's house. I'd never seen it before, but the address was right there on the white stucco wall next to the front door. It was a sharp, angular building, black and white, lots of windows, very modern. It wasn't anything like our house back in Oregon. It was built into the side of a hill, with oaks, maples, and birches all around it. It looked like someplace an artist would live, not a dentist. The carport was under the house, and I saw a black Mercedes parked there.

Before I could chicken out, and with my heart bonging away like an Indian drum, I walked up the curving steps to the front door. My drawing pad was tucked under my arm. I took a deep breath and punched the doorbell button. A muffled musical chime echoed behind the door. I heard dogs barking out back, and I wondered if they were the labs I had seen on the postcard. For a second, I was overcome with the urge to run, but I kept my feet cemented firmly in place.

I heard footsteps.

The click of a dead bolt.

The door opened.

A young woman about my height, with long curly black hair,

answered the door. She wore a white blouse and tan slacks. She was thin and pretty, not model pretty but close, with an oval face and bright green eyes, skin the color of milk. It took me a second to recognize her as the woman from Dad's postcards—she looked younger in person. I guessed she was in her mid-twenties, which would have made her twenty years younger than Dad. She wore a big fat diamond ring on her wedding finger. It was a least three times the size of the diamond in the ring Mom kept in the fish-shaped bowl in her bathroom.

"Can I hel—" she began, and then her eyes got wide. Her hand came up to cover her mouth. "Oh," she said. "Oh, you're—you're . . . I've seen your picture."

There was a lump in my throat that felt like a tennis ball. I swallowed it away.

"Charlie," I said.

"Right," she said. "Yes, you, um . . ."

"I was wondering . . ."

"If Jim is home?" she said. "He's already—already left for work. Just a few minutes ago. But come in. I'll call him on his cell. I'm—I'm Monica, by the way. I'm . . . Jim's wife." She said the last bit in a quieter voice, as if she was ashamed, suddenly, to admit it.

"Nice to meet you," I said.

"Come in, come in," she said, and stepped aside. "Jim said you might show up here. He—your mom talked to him. She told us."

I wasn't surprised Mom had given Dad advanced warning, but I was still irritated. I walked into an entryway with a maroon-colored tiled floor, brightly lit from the skylights above us. Monica stepped over to a white marble table and picked up an antique black phone. But before she dialed, a toddler with blond pigtails appeared in the doorway that led down the hall. The kid wore pink shorts and a Dora the Explorer T-shirt. She carried a stuffed purple alligator under one arm, and she was sucking on a thumb. She couldn't have been more than two.

"Oh," Monica said, putting the phone back in the cradle. "Charlie, this is Evette. Our daughter."

I knew before she spoke who the little girl was. And it changed everything. I don't know why, but it did. I felt like I'd walked into the house only to have a trapdoor open underneath me.

"Hi," I said. My voice sounded funny.

The girl went on sucking her thumb. Monica laughed nervously and picked up the phone again, dialing quickly. The little girl and I just stared at each other. Her big eyes made her look like a teddy bear. Monica was saying something about me, saying I was right there, right there in the foyer, waiting, but it seemed like it was coming from far away. It was just me and this little girl. My sister. My *half* sister.

"Charlie," Monica said.

I flinched. She stood right next to me. I hadn't noticed that she was off the phone.

"I'm sorry," she said.

"It's okay," I said.

"Jim—your dad. He's on his way. He'll—he'll be here in just a minute."

"Okay."

"Do you ... do you want something? Something to drink? Have you had breakfast? I can make you something. Eggs? A waffle?"

166

"I'm okay," I said.

"Are you sure? Because it's really no trouble."

"No, I'll just wait."

"All right. If you're sure."

"I'm sure."

She looked like she wanted to say something else, but instead she just smiled weakly and looked at the floor. Truth was, my stomach felt like a vacuum that would suck in all the food in the house, but I was too nervous to eat. If I did, I'd just throw up. I looked back at the little girl. Evette. Dad's little girl. And then I knew why it bothered me so much, seeing her. I'd come all this way to give Dad a portrait, but I had a portrait in my head, too, a picture of the way his life would be when I found him. I hadn't drawn kids into that picture. I hadn't expected him to want any more. I hadn't expected him to want to replace me.

"Oh," Monica said, suddenly concerned, "oh, oh . . . do you— do you want a tissue?" She hurried over to the little table where the phone sat and snatched up a box of tissues, one in a fake white marble box that perfectly matched the color of the table. She thrust it at me. "Here. Here, please."

I didn't realize why she was acting so strange until I tasted the salty tear touching my lips. I touched my cheek and felt the wetness there. I'd started crying and I hadn't even realized it.

Ashamed, I took a tissue and wiped my cheek. I avoided her eyes. "Thanks," I said in a quiet voice.

She must have been embarrassed at me crying, because she scooped up the little girl. "I have to change Evette," she said. "I—you can wait in the living room right there. He'll—he'll be here in a minute." She started to leave, then turned back. "Just yell if you need anything, okay? Just yell."

With that, she was gone. I thought about leaving. I was caught in the limbo world exactly between wanting to stay and wanting to go, which prevented me from doing anything at all. I just stood there in the entryway, not moving an inch from where Monica had left me, still holding the tissue in my hand. I heard the distant sounds of a television down the hall. It may have been there before, but I hadn't noticed it. They were cartoon voices, and they sounded familiar. *Sesame Street?* Yeah, I heard Oscar. The girl had been watching *Sesame Street* when I came in. I had loved *Sesame Street* as a kid.

At some point I must have drifted into the living room, because I found myself sitting in a wicker chair, staring at the tissue cupped between my hands. Next to me was a black grand piano, the top up. Leather-bound books lined the far wall. The wall near the entryway was entirely made of floor-to-ceiling windows.

I heard a car pull up outside. A door open and shut. Footsteps on the concrete. I heard the front door open.

"Monica?"

Dad's voice sounded different over the phone, so different that for a moment I thought it wasn't him.

"Monica?" he said. "Are you here?"

I didn't say anything. I didn't know what to say. My heart rattled away like a machine gun. I heard the door close. I heard him walking on the tiles. I looked up, holding my breath, waiting for him to round the corner. Finally, his bearded face appeared as he ducked his head into the room, scanning it, looking for his wife. He started to turn away when he must have realized what he'd seen, then he turned back sharply.

"Oh," he said.

He stayed there, head in the room, body out, as if he was afraid to come all the way inside. When I was little, he used to let his beard get all woolly, and Mom and I called him Papa Bear, but now it was neatly trimmed. There was a lot of gray in it that hadn't been there before, and his hairline had receded so that his forehead looked much bigger. He used to wear thick glasses, but he wasn't wearing them now. I wondered if he had contacts or if he'd had laser surgery.

Finally, he stepped into the room, looking uncomfortable, looking like he wanted to be somewhere else. He wore charcoal-gray slacks, a blue-and-white Hawaiian shirt, and black leather loafers. He was a big guy, big and wide-shouldered like a football linebacker, and he was heavier around the middle than when I'd seen him last. I couldn't remember when I'd seen him last. Three years? Four? He'd come out to take me camping for a week, but it had rained, so we had packed it in early. He had gone home after four days, saying he'd make it up to me later.

"Charlie," he said.

"Hi, Dad," I said.

He seemed to recover a little, his face growing stern. "I'm very surprised at you, Charlie. I can't believe you'd do this. Do you know how much your mother's been worrying? She wanted to call the police, but I told her to wait a few days." He shook his head. "I never thought you'd pull a stunt like this."

A stunt. He was calling my appearance a stunt. He hadn't

seen me in person in years, hadn't talked to me on the phone in months, and when he sees me, it's a stunt. I didn't know what to say. I'd come a thousand miles, and I didn't have anything to say. So I just opened the drawing pad in my lap, took out Dad's portrait, and handed it to him.

He took it, his brow furrowing. "What's this?"

"It's a picture of you."

"I can see that."

I waited for him to say something else. Maybe something about how good it was, how much talent I had. He looked at the picture a long time, or at least what seemed like a long time, and I wanted to read a lot into that, him looking at it, thinking maybe it was so good he couldn't pry his eyes away, but then he handed it back to me.

I was so surprised by this that I didn't know what to say. At best, I had expected him to ask me if he could have it. At worst, I had expected him to say I should be spending my time doing more serious things, like studying. I hadn't expected him to merely hand it to me without saying anything. I thought about telling him it wasn't finished yet, I was still working on it, still had a few more last touches to make, but he spoke before I had a chance.

"I need to call your mother," he said. "I need to tell her you're here, that you're okay. Then we'll talk about how to get you home."

He nodded at me and turned and walked away. That's all I got? A nod, the way a general nods to his soldier? I felt a flare of anger, hot and fierce, but then just as quickly, it was gone. It was gone and my insides were like a fallen leaf left too long in the sun, dried up and brittle. If you reached inside me and squeezed, it might all crumble to nothing.

I heard him pick up the phone and dial. I heard him talking to Mom. Yes, he's here. Yes, yes, we'll get him home. . . . Next flight. . . . Sure. . . . No, I haven't asked him. . . . Yes, he looks fine. . . . Okay, I'll have him do that. There were lots of pauses between his answers, and then Dad said good-bye. I waited for him to re-enter the room, but instead I heard him call to Monica and then his footsteps.

There was lots more I should have done. I should have told Dad how much the picture meant to me, how I really wanted him to have it, maybe frame it, and put it on his office wall. I should have told him that I'd come a long way, and the least he could do was sit down and talk to me, treat me the way a father should treat a son, maybe tell me why he'd been pretty much AWOL in my life. There were questions that needed answers, and I deserved those answers. All I had to do was ask them. All I had to do was force him to deal with me instead of avoiding me.

But I couldn't.

Even coming a thousand miles, even after everything I'd been through to get there, I couldn't do any of that.

Without making too much noise, I left the drawing pad on the wicker chair and tiptoed back to the front door. I heard distant voices somewhere down the hall and then Evette's screech. I hesitated just for a second, then opened the door.

And ran.

chapter sixteen

Most people who'd ever seen me run—which was something I tried to avoid if at all possible—usually said I looked like I was about to fall down. When I ran as fast I could, which really wasn't all that fast, things got even worse. My legs and arms always seemed to be flailing like I was having a seizure. I ran down one street, then another, finally losing my balance and crashing on someone's front yard. The grass was wet, soaking the front of my shirt and pants, but I lay there anyway, choking in the thin Denver air.

"Charlie?"

I looked up, and there was Jake, materializing out of the morning sun like some kind of ghost, still dressed in a jean jacket and faded blue jeans.

"What are you doing, man?" he said.

I sat up, hugging my knees. An old man across the street who had been trimming his roses was staring at us. I didn't care.

"How'd you get here?" I asked.

"Hitchhiked. Wasn't all that hard, really. The interstate is less than a mile from here. I found your dad's place, and I was watching from the bushes across the street when I saw you run out of there all freaked out. What happened?"

"Saw Dad," I said.

"I guessed that. You give him the picture?"

"Yeah."

"What did he say?"

I told him what had happened. My voice sounded like someone else talking through a tape recorder. Jake's face grew darker, especially when I mentioned the little girl. When I was finished, he shook his head.

"You gotta go back there," he said.

"Nah."

"Charlie—"

"Not this time, Jake," I said. "I did what I needed to do."

"You can't let him ignore you, man."

"Why not?"

"Because it's wrong. Because he's your dad."

He may have been right, but I didn't care anymore. I didn't care about anything. I just wanted to go home, back to Mom and her soon-to-be-husband, Rick, and Leo Gonzalez and my Human Squid life. I wanted to go back and pretend none of this stuff had ever happened. I was going to say this to Jake, but then I remembered his own plan, to go see his uncle. Maybe I could delay going home just a little longer. Maybe helping him would be a way I could forget this whole mess.

"How about we go see Uncle Bruce?" I said.

"Huh?" he said. He stared at me blankly.

"In Cheyenne?"

"What? Oh right, right. Yeah, my uncle."

Suddenly I realized what I should have realized right from the first. "You made him up, didn't you?"

"What?"

"He doesn't exist."

"Sure he does!"

"Come on, Jake, admit it."

He turned and started walking. I got up and followed him. I wasn't going to let it drop. He had spit out one lie after another, and I wanted the truth. "Why'd you want to come here?" I said.

"I told you, two birds with one stone. Help you and help me."

"Okay, then let's go see your uncle."

"I changed my mind," Jake said. "I don't really think he's going to help me."

"Bullshit," I said.

"Think whatever you want," Jake said. "I'm just going to make it on my own."

"We don't have any money."

"Small problem. You really should go back to your dad, Charlie. He's going to be looking for you. You may not like him, but at least he's there waiting for you. At least he can help you get home. I can't help you at all." He pulled out a cigarette and lit it.

I had a flash of insight. "What happened with your dad?" I said.

He stopped and looked at me, the cigarette dangling limply from his mouth.

"What?" he said.

"Something happened with your dad."

"What are you talking about? I told you, he's a loser."

"Did he get married again?"

"I think you'd better drop it."

"Did he have a new kid, like my dad did?"

"Charlie—"

"Did he go to jail or something? Tell me. There's some reason you really want me to work things out with my dad. If you'd just tell me—"

"SHUT UP!"

He screamed it in my face and gave me a good shove. It wasn't enough to hurt me, but it did make me stagger backward. The look in his eyes made me realize that if I pressed it any more, he'd probably go berserk. He glared at me a little longer, then turned and stalked away. I followed, hanging back a few steps.

"Where are you going?" I asked.

"Go home," he said.

"My home is in Oregon."

"You know what I mean."

"I want to help you."

"Nobody can help me," Jake said. "Just leave me alone."

"What're you going to do?"

"I don't know. I need some money."

With a chill, I remembered the gun in his jacket pocket. I didn't want him to do anything stupid. "How?"

"I have an idea."

"Jake—"

"Don't worry, it's not something illegal. Well, not really."

"Jake, come on." I could clearly see the bulge of the gun in his inside jacket pocket, and it scared me, thinking of him using it. "You don't want to get arrested or anything."

"I'm not going to get arrested. Trust me, man. Go back to your dad. He'll get you back to Oregon."

"You should come with me," I said. "We'll go home together."

"I'm not going back there," Jake said. "I don't know what I'm going to do, but I'm not going back there."

I decided to stay with him. No way I was going to let him get into any serious trouble. If that was the only thing I accomplished on this trip, at least it would be something. I figured at any moment Dad would probably round the corner in his car, and then I'd be able to convince Jake to come with me.

Jake stopped at the driveway of a big brick house, dropping his cigarette and stubbing it out on the sidewalk.

"This should do," he said, smiling.

"What should do?"

"Just be quiet and let me do the talking."

Straightening his hair and smoothing out his clothes, he walked up the driveway to the doors. He rang the doorbell, then gave me a wink. After a moment, I heard movement inside the house. I saw a shadow pass by the colored opaque glass, and then the door opened. A middle-aged woman, her hair too blond to be real, answered the door.

"Yes?" she said.

"Hello, ma'am," Jake said, pitching his voice a little higher. "I'm Jimmy James Johnson of Denver Christian Academy, and I'm raising money to help send Bibles to poor children in Afghanistan. One five-dollar bill will pay for five Bibles, ma'am, at the discount the publisher's giving us. Would you like to donate? We sure could use your help."

I almost laughed. No way this would work. But sure enough, the woman went to get her purse, and Jake walked away from that house with a crisp new ten-dollar bill. We hit three more houses where people were home, and even though the guilt gnawed at me for taking people's money, I was blown away by how sincere Jake sounded with his spiel. Dad never showed up in his car. At the next house, a two-story white one with white pillars flanking the front steps, nobody answered, but Jake stopped when we were passing the garage.

"Whoa," he said.

He was looking into the dark windows of the garage doors. I stepped up next to him and saw what he saw: a shiny yellow Corvette.

"Yeah, it's nice," I said, and started to walk away. When I realized Jake wasn't joining me, I stopped. He was still standing there, cupping his hands on either side of his face so he could get a better look.

"I gotta drive it," he said.

"Oh no," I said.

"Oh yes," he said. "Come on, let's go back to the front door."

"There's no one home!"

"That's what I'm hoping," he said.

"What?"

He didn't answer. Following him, I glanced over my shoulder to see if anyone was watching. Luckily, the tall hedge in front of their yard shielded the house from all but a few houses across the street, and I didn't see anyone over there. Jake rang the doorbell again. When no one answered, he rapped on the door. Still no one came to the door. He smiled like a little gremlin and walked across the bark dust in front of the house, trying the windows as he went.

"Jake!" I said.

He brought a finger to his lips. "We'll just take it for a test drive around the block," he whispered. "They won't even know it."

"You can't do this!"

He disappeared around the corner of the house. I stood there a moment longer, hating that he was getting me into this, that we were going to add breaking and entering to our list of accomplishments, then sprinted after him. He was trying a smaller window on the back side, one with foggy glass, and when I got there, I saw the window slide open. He smiled at me. There was a high wooden fence that separated the house from the one next door, and I heard children playing in the backyard behind the neighbor's house. There was one tiny window on the neighbor's house, high up, and it was dark. I imagined someone standing there in the dark watching us. No way to know for sure.

Jake was already climbing into the house with the Corvette when I reached him.

"Don't!" I whispered urgently. "There might be an alarm."

"The window was cracked open already."

"It might be a motion detector."

He flopped through, landing with a grunt on the inside. "Don't think so," he said.

"Why's that?"

"'Cause there's a fluffy orange cat sitting in here, purring. She'd set off any alarm." His face appeared in the open window. "You coming or not?"

"No way," I said.

"Okay, suit yourself."

I watched him disappear from the bathroom out into a bedroom.

"Jake!" I called after him.

He didn't answer.

"Jake!"

Still nothing. I stood there, agonizing about the right thing to do. The kids next door were screeching and laughing, chasing each other around the yard from the sounds of it. A car passed on the street, out of my view, but it still made me drop to a crouch. I could just wait to see if Jake managed to get the keys to the Corvette, or I could go in and try to stop him. I had to get him out of that house. I'd gone with him on a joyride with Mr. Harkin's Mustang, but that had been a life-and-death thing, a way to avoid getting my face ripped off by Leo. This wasn't at all the same. I had visions of dozens of police cars showing up at any minute, triggered by a silent alarm. If I stayed outside, I was innocent of any wrongdoing, but then I was leaving Jake high and dry.

I had to stop him.

It took a bit of effort, but I managed to struggle into the house, landing on a plush bathroom mat in the dark bathroom, lit only from the daylight coming from the window. When I turned, I looked right into the glowing eyes of an orange tabby, and I let out a little yelp. The cat cocked its head at me and purred.

I tiptoed quickly into a huge master bedroom, past a four-poster bed and ornate, dark-stained furniture littered with junk. I saw a person approaching me from across the room, and froze, terrified, then realized it was my own reflection in a mirror. A voice in my head screamed, *You shouldn't be here!* Heart pounding,

I walked through a dark hall and into a living room with a high vaulted ceiling, the skylights and the glass patio doors filling the room with natural light. It seemed very empty, with a tan couch and a grand piano down at one end, the rest of the hardwood floor covered only by a rug that made me think of one of those mandala pictures Tibetan monks create, the ones with all the intricate geometrical patterns.

I was about to continue into what looked like the dining room when I finally noticed Jake on the other side of the piano, his back to me. The propped-open piano lid was practically blocking him from view.

"Jake!" I whispered.

He didn't answer. I walked toward him and saw that he was staring at the silver-framed pictures decorating the wall.

"Jake, we have to get out of here," I said. Even whispering, my voice echoed in the cavernous room.

Still, he didn't say anything. I stepped up next to him. I noticed that he was looking at one picture in particular, a large one in the center of the others that showed three people standing on a wooden bridge in front of a waterfall—a man, a woman, and a smiling teenage boy who looked about our age.

"You know them?" I said.

Jake shook his head.

"Jake," I said, "we really should—"

"They look happy," Jake said finally. "You think they look happy?"

I looked at the picture again. They did look happy, but not any more than anyone else in front of a camera, their smiles plastic, their eyes dull. "I guess," I said. "But we need to get out—"

"My dad's dead," Jake said.

His voice was so flat that at first I thought he might be joking, but then he burst into tears. It was such a violent outburst of emotion, especially for Jake, that I stood there paralyzed, watching him. He sobbed like a little boy, a wail that would have woken anyone in the house if there had been anyone there. I didn't know what to do. I didn't know if I should try to comfort him or try to pretend I hadn't noticed. In the end, I didn't have to decide, because he turned to me and hugged me, burying his face in my shirt.

"Hey," I said. "Hey, man, it's all right."

While he cried, I patted him on the back, so overwhelmed by his outpouring of emotion that I even forgot to be awkward and embarrassed at hugging another boy. Having your dad die was rough, no matter what kind of father he'd been.

"Died . . . in a . . . bar fight," Jake said between shuddering breaths. "Found out . . . last week."

"Oh man, I'm sorry," I said.

"I . . . hate him. *Hate* him."

"Okay."

"I wish he'd never been born."

I held him until the crying stopped. Sniffling, he pulled away from me, wiping at his eyes.

"Sorry," he said.

"Don't worry about it."

"You probably think I'm a total wuss."

"Nah."

"I just thought, I don't know, if we saw your dad . . ."

He didn't finish the sentence, just ending it with a little shrug, but something clicked in my head anyway and I finally understood Jake a little better. As much as he said he hated his father, he'd probably been hoping for years that his dad would come home and make things right. That his dad would patch their lives back together and they'd be a family again. It didn't make any sense, but I knew it was true because I felt it too sometimes, the hope that some miracle would occur that would magically make my parents get back together and put our lives back where they had been before, as if nothing had happened. That's why it had been so important to him that I see my dad. He was hoping I could have what he couldn't—even if deep down he must have known, just as I did, that it was impossible.

"Jake—" I began.

"Hey!"

It was a shout from across the room, and we both jerked back as if a bomb had exploded between us. I turned and there was this kid, this twenty-year-old kid, wild-eyed and half-naked, standing on the other side of the room. He was skinny and tall, barefoot, dressed in blue boxers and a white tank top. His eyes were blood-shot, no white in them at all, just pink, and he had what looked like dried blood around one nostril. He was so thin and wasted that it took me a second to realize it was the same kid as in the picture.

"Whatareyoudoinginmyhouse?" The kid's words all ran together, slurred and barely understandable.

Jake raised his hands. "We're leaving," he said. "We're leaving right now."

"I'mgonnakillyou!" the kid said.

"Wait a minute—" Jake started.

But the kid lowered his head and charged like a bull. Jake and I ran behind the piano, and the kid followed, screaming. We circled around the piano and headed out of the room, me right on Jake's heels. Then I was tackled from behind. My nose smashed into the carpet, making my eyes water.

Before I could get my wits about me, the kid grabbed my hair and started ramming my face into the carpet, him still screaming the whole time. I tasted blood in my mouth. The world started to go dark. Then I heard Jake shout and felt the kid go tumbling off of me.

The world spinning, my ears ringing, I was only vaguely aware of what was happening around me, but I heard the sounds of struggle. Something glass or ceramic fell to the floor and smashed. I managed to roll over and sit up, blinking through tears and sweat, and saw Jake throwing the kid against the wall. Two decorative plates fell from the wall and smashed to the hardwood floor. The earlier sound had come from a white vase that had been sitting on an end table and fallen to the floor as well.

The kid was crumpled over on himself, on his back, his legs over his body, and he lay there dazed and panting.

"Just—just stay there!" Jake cried. There was a red jagged gash that looked like lightning on his neck. The front of his shirt was torn straight down the middle, exposing his bony ribs.

The kid shook his head like he was trying to throw off his confusion. "Gonnakillyouasshole!" he shouted.

This is the part where we were supposed to run. But Jake didn't do that. He jerked the gun out of his pocket and pointed it at the kid. I heard the click of the safety. It was like the world suddenly changed, everything becoming quiet. Even the kid's heavy breathing stopped, his bloodshot eyes growing wide.

"Now listen," Jake said. "We're leaving. You just let us go."

"Jake—" I said.

"Shut up, Charlie," Jake said. He never looked away from the kid. "We're leaving, you understand? We're leaving and you're just gonna sit there."

Jake started to back away. For a moment, the kid just glared at us, and I thought he was actually going to let us go. Jake glanced at me and was about to say something when the kid let out a shriek that didn't even sound human and, in a wild flailing of arms and legs, came charging at Jake again. The gun came up, and I thought, *Here it comes, it's going to go off*, but Jake didn't fire. The kid plowed into him and they went down right at my feet, the gun clattering to the floor.

"Gonnakillyougonnakillyougonnakillyou!" the kid screamed.

The kid let loose with a hurricane of blows, pummeling Jake on his face and chest. Jake raised his arms, trying to resist, trying to protect himself, but the onslaught was overpowering, like trying to fight an ocean wave. I yelled for the kid to stop, but he went on punching, and Jake's face got redder. His neck got rubbery, like there were no bones in it anymore, and his face bounced from side to side with each blow. The kid was going to kill Jake. He was going to kill him right in front of me.

I did the only thing I could do to stop it. I lunged for the gun. I picked it up. I pointed it at the kid.

"Stop!" I shouted. "Stop or I'll shoot!"

There must have been something in my voice, something that penetrated the kid's madness, because the frenzy stopped. The kid, breathing hard, fists bloodied, turned and looked at me. Jake, his face a mess, let out a little moan and his head rolled a little side to side.

"Now—now you just let him go," I said. My voice warbled and my voice felt tight. The gun trembled in my hand. I didn't know what I was doing. I'd never even held a gun, much less fired one. "Just—just let him go."

The kid stared at me, breathing through his nose like some kind of beast. There are moments when your life spins on a wheel, when the choices you make forever change the person you are and the person you will become. I got into Mr. Harkin's Mustang and life was never the same, never would be the same. Now I held a gun and my finger was on the trigger. I could feel the rest of the world disappearing around me. It was just me, the kid, and Jake. And the gun. The gun, cold and heavy, was the only thing that still felt real. Something was happening. The wheel was spinning. Something was going to change.

Then, with a cry, the kid leaped from Jake and charged.

He charged straight at me. There was murderous rage in his eyes. He was charging, and I moved back, but he was so much faster, so wild and crazy, this monster that was once a boy.

He was almost on me.

His fingers scraped my shirt.

The gun fired.

chapter
seventeen

I have no memory of pulling the trigger. It must have happened, but I simply don't remember doing it. There was a loud bang, and my hand jerked back as if somebody had slammed into the front of the gun with a baseball bat. For a second I thought the gun had missed, because the kid kept charging. But in the next second I saw the burst of blood in the middle of the kid's chest, and I saw his expression change from rage to stunned amazement. It was the first time he had actually looked human. He was still moving forward, but his legs gave out from under him, and he went down, bumping against my legs, throwing me against the wall. There was a haze in the air, and I smelled it, the bitter sting of gun smoke.

I was babbling, saying I didn't mean to, it was an accident, but my voice wasn't making any sound. Then I realized that I heard no sound at all, that the world had gone completely silent.

The kid lay facedown on the floor, half on the rug and half on the hardwood, the blood seeping out of him like a living thing, an ooze that was expanding, seeking, hungry. I might have screamed, but since I couldn't hear it, I may have only imagined that I screamed.

Murderer.

The word leaped into my mind. It wasn't my voice saying it. It was Dad. It was Dad calling me a murderer. I don't know how long I stood there looking down at the body, but eventually I felt someone shaking me. I looked up and there was Jake, looking like a boxer after twelve rounds in the ring with a much tougher opponent, face puffy and red, one eye swollen shut. His bloodied lips were moving, but it took awhile to realize he was speaking, that there were words coming out of his mouth.

". . . out of it, Charlie," he said. "Snap out of it. Come on, give me the gun. Just give it to me. Easy now. Slowly. There you go."

I felt him pry the gun from my fingers. The fingers didn't feel like they were mine. They felt as if they were attached, but they didn't belong to me.

"I shot him," I said.

"I know," Jake said.

"I shot him."

"You had to. He was drugged up pretty good, out of his mind. Now come on, man. We'll call an ambulance when we're out of here."

He turned to go, but I didn't move. I couldn't move even if I wanted to. I was a statue. My feet were glued to the ground.

"Charlie?" Jake said.

"Is he dead?"

"I don't know. Probably. Come on—"

"I can't leave."

"Charlie!"

I shook my head. "I can't leave. Not now. Got to . . . call an ambulance. Stay here. Shot him. It's—it's my fault." I started toward the other room, waking in a daze, wondering where a phone might be.

"Charlie, come on!" He grabbed at my shirt, trying to pull me after him, and I tore myself away.

"No, Jake!"

And for the first time, I heard a siren in the distance, closing. Jake's eyes got wider, and his tone got more frantic.

"No good will come from staying here!" he shouted. "You'll just end up in prison, ruining your life. Think!"

"No," I said.

"There's nothing you can do! If he's still alive, they'll help him. If he's dead, he's dead. Don't throw your life away."

"No, Jake." While his voice had become shrill, my own sounded hollow and defeated. I didn't feel any great moral certainty in what I was saying; I just knew I couldn't leave. I had to stay.

The sirens became louder, a block away now, maybe two. Jake paced back and forth, shaking his head, and then looked at me. I'd never really seen him look scared, but now he did.

"All right, listen," he said. "Listen to me. I have the gun. I'm going to say I shot him."

"No," I said, "you don't have to—"

"Listen to me! Your life is going somewhere. Mine's already in the toilet."

"Jake—"

"Shut up!"

The sirens were much louder now, and there was more than one. I heard the screech of tires.

"We couldn't run now if we wanted," he said. "They'll be here in a second. I shot him, okay? He was going to kill you, and I shot him. I shot him in self-defense."

"It'll never—"

"Just shut up!" he said. Amid all the blood and bruises, there were tears streaming down his face. "Just shut the hell up, okay! I'm going to do this! You're going to go to college and have a life and do great stuff! I'm not taking that away from you. You just let me do this! I can do this thing!"

I heard the slamming of car doors. Shouts outside. Someone was banging on the front door.

"Why?" I said to Jake.

"Because—" he began, and swallowed hard. "Because I can. Because it's something I can do."

We stood looking at each other, and I should have said something, I should have argued, but then there was a crash and the police were in the house, a swarm of blue uniforms. Jake was disarmed and pushed to the floor. I was shoved against a wall. The handcuffs came out, snapped closed. The rights were read. A crackle of radios. Shouts. A tornado of activity closed in on us, but we were in the eye, Jake and me, and there was a moment, before we were hauled away, that our gazes locked. I wanted to say something right then. I wanted to shout out that I did it, I shot the kid, but Jake's eyes stopped me.

Don't take this away from me, he was saying. *Don't you dare take this away from me.*

chapter eighteen

We waited in the little room until my name was called, and then we filed into the courtroom, Mom on one side and Dad on the other. It was weird, because it felt like we were a family, even though I knew better. The last five months, the three of us had spent so much time together you'd think we were a family again, but we had never actually walked like this, the three of us together, a parent on each side. It seemed much more real that way. That's what families did. They sometimes walked together. Of course, not many families walked together into a murder trial.

"Now just remember," Mom said, squeezing my arm, "you just tell the truth and everything will be fine."

She was dressed all in black, like maybe she thought she was going to a funeral. Dad wore a dark blue suit, similar to the suit I was wearing. He'd bought it for me. He'd said blue was a good color if you were testifying, because people were more likely to believe you if you were a man and you were wearing blue. I wondered how he knew such a thing was true, but not enough that I actually asked. There'd been a lot of stuff I'd wanted to say lately, but it was as if my mouth had been shut off and my body was running on autopilot. The real me was someplace else.

I couldn't be here. If I was here, I'd have to think about what I'd done.

I was okay until they opened the paneled doors and I saw

all the people sitting in the rows, and up front, behind that big wooden desk, the judge in black. My heart started pounding like crazy, and it got even worse when I saw Jake in the orange prison uniform at the table to the left. It was just the back of his head, but I knew it was him. He was the only one in the room who hadn't turned to look at me.

Even in a big city like Denver, the story of our break-in and the shooting was front-page stuff, mostly because we were juveniles so far from home. And of course, the *Rexton Times* back home had been running articles regularly on it since it had happened, or so Mom had said. I hadn't actually left Denver since I was released on bail.

So far, they were only charging me with breaking and entering, and there was a deal in place that as long as I testified that Jake had shot the kid, they wouldn't charge me with anything else. Dad's expensive lawyer had helped a bunch on that account. I would probably serve a couple of months in juvie when it was all said and done, but that would be it. I'd already spent a few days in jail right after it had happened. Somehow I could get through a few months without losing my mind.

My parents took their seats on the aisle, and I walked alone to the front, where an officer of the court asked me to put my hand on the Bible and swear to tell the truth, the whole truth, and nothing but the truth, so help me God. I heard my own voice saying the words back, and it sounded like it was coming back to me from the end of a long tunnel.

The whole truth.

As much as I had tried to put the shooting out of my mind, it was all I could think about the last few months, as the case went from advisement, to hearing, to arraignment, and finally to trial, the district attorney pushing it through as fast as possible, me learning more than I had ever wanted to know about our justice system. The truth. I'd gone over and over what had happened that day in my mind, trying to see some way to stop what had happened. I never should have gone into the house, but if I hadn't gone in, Jake might be dead instead of the kid. Wayne Tolley. He had a name. I didn't want to use his name, because it hurt to even think it. He'd been in and out of drug rehabs since he was fourteen, his dad a widowed importer who spent a lot of time abroad. They'd found more than twenty ounces of cocaine in the kid's room. Jake had been right. The kid had been drugged out of his mind.

He hadn't deserved to die, though, no matter what kind of state of mind he had been in, and I was the one who'd shot him. Me, Charlie Hill, a killer. There was no getting over it. I was the one who had shot him and Jake was going to pay for it. He'd said he wanted to take the fall, that I should let him do it, but then why hadn't he confessed? He'd pleaded not guilty. Maybe he thought he could get off on a technicality, but I didn't see how he could prove he wasn't guilty. They had him standing over a dead body with the weapon in his hand. Like the prosecutor had said in the paper, it was a slam dunk. They were even trying him as an adult, which they could do in Colorado. It was going to be brutal.

I took my seat on the witness stand. Elevated, and surrounded by wooden walls, I felt like I was on a ship, and all the people sitting out there were just faces bobbing in the sea. The people in the jury box were staring at me as if they were trying to read my thoughts.

I glanced up at the judge, who was small and weaselly, his glasses so heavy it seemed his nose might break from the weight of them, not at all the way I imagined a judge should look. A judge should look like God.

". . . confirm for the jury that you were with the defendant, Jonathon Tucker, at the time Wayne Tolley was shot and killed?"

It took me a moment to realize that the prosecutor—a tall man with thin brown slicked-back hair, the kind of guy who looked like he should be selling Oldsmobiles with bad tires instead of putting kids behind bars—was speaking to me. My throat felt scratchy, and I swallowed several times.

"Yes sir," I said.

"Can you point to Jonathon Tucker, please?"

I raised my finger and pointed. Jake still wasn't looking at me, his gaze fixed on the blank yellow legal pad in front of him. Strangely, he looked more clean-cut and presentable as a prisoner than he ever had before, his hair short and neatly trimmed, his face clean and free of stubble. However, he did look even thinner, if that was possible, and his eyes had recessed into deep sockets. I could only imagine the hell he'd been through the past few months. His foster parents hadn't even come for him. He was totally on his own.

The whole truth.

The prosecutor was talking now, reminding the jury of what had happened, and my supposed part in it, and I was sure this was all a lead-up to asking me the big question. He would ask me if I had seen Jake shoot the kid. It was the question I'd been waiting months to answer. I'd written down what I was going to say, word for word, spending hours memorizing it, knowing that there was a good chance I'd blow it all if I tried to make it up on the spot. The first few times I recited it (quietly in my room at Dad's house, late, when everyone was asleep), I'd felt like throwing up, but it had gotten easier the more times I'd said it.

But now that I was looking at Jake, all the shame and regret came rushing right back, just as it had right after I'd shot the kid. My stomach churned and the acid burned in my throat. I'd shot the kid. I'd shot someone. After I had pulled that trigger, the world was different, I was different, and I didn't know if I'd ever be able to get back to living a somewhat normal life. Even if everyone else could get past this, I didn't know if I ever would. It would forever define me, just like being left-handed or a Taurus defined you. I didn't want to throw away my life. I didn't want to go to jail. But how could I let Jake take the fall for me?

It was right then, sitting in that courtroom, that I finally realized something. I realized that Jake was a better person than me.

He may have been a smoker, a troublemaker, a dropout, and even a lawbreaker when it suited him, but he was a better person. He was a *good* person. What he'd done with Anju and her mom, what he'd done to help me see Dad, those were *good* things. They were things that mattered, that made a difference. He'd done more good stuff in one week than I'd done in my entire life. He was a good person, and what was I? I was a nothing. I'd never risked myself in any way for other people. Here I was doing it again, taking the cowardly path. I was letting Jake take the fall for me because it saved me. I'd lobbed the water balloon that had done the most damage, and now Jake was going to take credit for it to save my ass.

I'd been trying to convince myself that maybe it was all right for Jake to take the fall because of the type of person he was, that maybe this sort of thing would have caught up to him eventually, but looking at him now, so alone at that table, I couldn't buy it anymore. Jake was not only a better person than me, I was hardly a person at all. I was hardly even there.

". . . you tell me, Charlie, did you see Mr. Tucker shoot the victim?"

I looked at the lawyer. So the moment had finally arrived. His mouth was open, as if he expected me to answer with a simple yes, and then he would proceed directly to the next question.

I may not have learned much in my sixteen years, but I have learned this: Life can turn on a wheel. It can. There are moments that come along that can change how things will play out for the rest of your life. But here's the thing. Here's the thing I've learned. Those moments come again and again. You may blow it once, but you almost always get another chance. The wheel just keeps on spinning. It's never too late to see if you might make something of yourself.

"I did it," I said.

The lawyer blinked. "Excuse me?"

"I did it," I said, louder, more sure of myself now. "I shot him."

"Damn it, Charlie!" Jake cried from where he was sitting.

"I SHOT HIM!" I shouted again, and it was like the cage doors opened and I was setting myself free. "IT'S MY FAULT!"

Pandemonium broke out in the courtroom, some shouts, a few

gasps. The judge banged his gavel and yelled for order. I just went on saying, *I did it!* I went on saying it and saying it, afraid that if I stopped, they'd pretend they hadn't heard me, and I didn't want people ignoring me, not this time, not now.

I was changing things, and nobody was going to stop me.

chapter nineteen

It was one of the hottest days of the summer, cracking a hundred degrees for the third straight day. Augusts in Rexton were usually hot and dry, but this was worse. This was like trying to live inside an oven.

Most of the students at Rexton Community College had taken refuge inside the air-conditioned brick buildings, leaving the campus deserted. I sat in the shade of a dogwood tree on the South Lawn, my drawing pad in my lap, a tin container of colored pencils on the grass next to me. The assignment was open-ended, just do something in color and something fast, so I could have done it indoors, but I wanted to tackle the Pioneer Fountain. In the eight months I'd been going to school, I'd already drawn it three times, but I still hadn't gotten it right.

It'd been over a year since I'd gotten out of prison back in Denver. The four years I'd spent in there hadn't been total hell, but they had been pretty close, especially when they had transferred me to the adult prison when I had turned eighteen. It had been a minimum-security-type work farm out in the flat farmlands, but it was still a prison even if there weren't any bars. You always knew there were bars even if you couldn't see them.

But I didn't get life in prison. I didn't get anything even close to that. It turned out that Dad's expensive lawyer had been worth the money. Even though the prosecutor was out for blood, the jury believed my story, that I *had* gone into the house to stop Jake, and that I had shot mostly in self-defense. It was still second-degree murder, but I only got seven years, and I got three years shaved off because of good behavior. At twenty-one, I was still older than most of the freshman community college students, but not by that much, not so much that anyone could tell.

"Hey there," a voice said behind me.

I knew the voice even before I turned. I knew the voice belonged to Jake Tucker, a voice I hadn't actually heard since he yelled, "Damn it, Charlie!" at the trial. What I *hadn't* expected was how he looked—trim and tan, thin but in a good way, a muscular way, his hair short, his blue polo shirt and tan slacks bright and clean. He stood there looking down at me, his hands shoved into his pockets, a gold watch glittering on his wrist. If it weren't for the crooked smirk, I wouldn't have known it was him. In fact, of the two of us, I was the one who looked more out there, having grown my hair long and taken to wearing paint-stained T-shirts and jeans with holes in them.

"Holy cow," I said.

"No thanks," he said. "I'm actually a vegetarian now."

I got to my feet, dusting off the grass and dirt. We shook hands, and then awkwardly gave each other a little hug and a pat on the back.

"Man, look at you," I said. "You got all respectable."

Jake shrugged. "After I got out of jail, I moved to LA and cleaned up my act. I'm actually in the entertainment business, can you believe it? Just a lowly assistant to a production assistant, which is just another way of saying coffee boy, but it's a start."

"Wow," I said.

"Sorry I didn't come sooner. I wanted to, but . . ." He shrugged.

We'd exchanged a couple of letters while we were both in our respective juvie prisons, but I hadn't heard from him since. "No big deal," I said.

"So, doing the art thing after all?" he said.

I nodded.

"Going to make a career out of it?" he asked.

"Yep."

"Cool. Bet your dad wasn't too happy about that."

I laughed. "I'm beyond caring what my dad thinks anymore."

He laughed, and then we were both laughing, and then just for a moment, it was like old times. At any moment one of us could have made a farting noise or crack a joke about jockstraps or panty lines. It lasted only a second, but it made me happy, knowing that those kids were still in us somewhere.

"Damn, it's hot," he said, tugging at his collar. "How can you even stand to be out here?"

"It builds character," I said.

"Yeah, okay, whatever." He looked away for a second, then, without looking at me, held up something that had been wrapped in newspaper. It was so small I hadn't even noticed it. "Got you something."

"Oh man, you didn't have to do that."

"Just take it," he said. "It's not what you . . . oh, just open it, okay?"

I ripped off the newspaper. Knowing Jake, or at least the *old*

Jake, I expected a gag gift, a rubber chicken or a noisemaker, but it wasn't anything like that at all. It was small and white, with a tiny screen, and at first I thought it was a cell phone or an iPod. Then I realized what it was, and I laughed.

"A Game Boy!" I said.

"Yeah," he said sheepishly. "I owed you one. Got it on eBay. It's . . . it's the same as the one you had before." He hesitated and then plunged ahead quickly. "You were right, Charlie. I broke yours. I . . . I wanted to tell you that. It's been bugging me."

I didn't know what to say. I hadn't thought about the Game Boy in a long time, but obviously Jake had. It was funny, how something could bother you for so long and then you just ended up forgetting about it.

There was so much more I wanted to say. I wanted to tell him that I was glad I had gotten into the Mustang with him. I wanted to tell him that I was glad I'd gone on that road trip and glad that I'd stayed on it all the way until the end. I wasn't glad about the Tolley kid dying. I'd had a lot of sleepless nights thinking about that one, plus plenty of sessions with the counselors, and it would always be a part of me. But it wasn't the only part of me. Something had happened during all of that, something that had made me finally realize it was up to me to do something with my life, to be somebody who did things rather than somebody who things just happened to. I wasn't going to be any doctor. I wanted to be an artist, and I really didn't care if anybody else approved.

But I didn't know how to put any of that into words. So much time had passed, and we were so different now, that it didn't seem to matter. I had a good feeling Jake already knew everything I would have said anyway.

"Well," he said.

He shuffled his feet. Where could we go from here? Then a couple of girls in tank tops and shorts walked by on the sidewalk path, and then I knew. "I got an idea," I said.

"Yeah?"

I pointed to the student union and started walking down the grassy hill. He fell into step next to me, our shadows small beneath us, as if they were trying to hide from the blazing sun.

"You know," I said, "I'm pretty sure they sell latex balloons in the bookstore."

He gave me the Jake smirk. "Oh really?"

"Yeah. I think it's time for the Water Balloon Boys to ride again."

"I think you're right," Jake said. And then, after a moment, he added, "Aren't you afraid of getting caught? I don't want to get you into trouble at your new school."

"Trouble?" I said, with plenty of fake dismay. "You think I'm worried about getting into trouble? You're such a dork."

"Double dork," he shot back.

"Dork on a stick!"

"Dork on a stick with a turd on top!" he cried.

We burst into a run, then, both of us laughing, racing toward the student union. The few people outdoors stared at us as if we were freaks, but I didn't mind. We *were* freaks, and it felt good. I suddenly remembered the time in Bend almost five years earlier, on a deserted street in the dead of night, and Jake had asked me a question I'd struggled to answer. *Are you happy?* Running now, the sun hot on my neck, my thoughts only on which bathroom would be best to fill up the water balloons in, I wanted to shout out the answer. I wanted to shout out that your life could be in the toilet, bad things could happen to you, and you could be depressed a lot of the time, but you could still say yes. You could still say yes and mean it. And if you meant it, if you really meant it, it might just be true.